A SOLDIER'S DAUGHTER

EV

Focusing on novels with contemporary concerns, Bantam New Fiction introduces some of the most exciting voices at work today. Look for these titles wherever Bantam New Fiction is sold:

BANTAM NEW FICTION

A SOLDIER'S DAUGHTER
NEVER CRIES

KAYLIE JONES

BANTAM BOOKS
NEW YORK • TORONTO • LONDON • SYDNEY • AUCKLAND

A SOLDIER'S DAUGHTER NEVER CRIES
A Bantam Book / July 1990

Grateful acknowledgment is made to the following for permission to reprint previously published material: "Rocky Raccoon" by John Lennon and Paul McCartney, copyright ©
1968, 1969 Northern Songs Ltd. All rights for the U.S., Canada and Mexico controlled and administered by EMI Blackwood Music, Inc. Under license from ATV Music (MAClen). All rights reserved. International copyright secured. Used by permission. "Autobiographia Literatia" by Frank O'Hara, copyright © 1967 by Maureen Granville-Smith, Administratrix of the Estate of Frank O'Hara. Reprinted from The Collected Poems of Frank O'Hara, *by permission of Alfred A. Knopf, Inc.*

Published simultaneously in hardcover and trade paperback editions.

A Soldier's Daughter Never Cries *orginally appeared in a different form in* Confrontation *#30-31 (November 1985).*

Library of Congress Cataloging-in-Publication Data

Jones, Kaylie, 1960–
    A soldier's daughter never cries / Kaylie Jones. —Bantam ed.
      p. cm.—(Bantam new fiction)
    ISBN 0-553-07017-7. —ISBN 0-553-34930-9 (pbk.)
    I. Title.
PS3560.O497S6 1990
813'.54—dc20   90-32655
                                                CIP

Published simultaneously in the United States and Canada

Bantam Books are published by Bantam Books, a division of Bantam Doubleday Dell Publishing Group, Inc. Its trademark, consisting of the words "Bantam Books" and the portrayal of a rooster, is Registered in U.S. Patent and Trademark Office and in other countries. Marca Registrada. Bantam Books, 666 Fifth Avenue, New York, New York 10103.

PRINTED IN THE UNITED STATES OF AMERICA

FG   0 9 8 7 6 5 4 3 2 1

To my brother Jamie

I would like to thank my oldest friend, James Bruce, for reminding me of how terrible I was when we were four years old,

and Joy Harris, my agent, who is as sensitive as she is tough.

Autobiographia Literaria

When I was a child
I played by myself in a
corner of the schoolyard
all alone.

I hated dolls and I
hated games, animals were
not friendly and birds
flew away.

If anyone was looking
for me I hid behind a
tree and cried out "I am
an orphan."

And here I am, the
center of all beauty!
writing these poems!
Imagine!

—Frank O'Hara

CONTENTS

THE SUITCASE

I remember the day my brother was brought to our house from the children's home, and everything is tinted a lemony yellow. This is not unusual, for I see my momentous childhood memories as though through colored lenses. Red, I identify with illnesses, high fevers, and summer heat. I learned to ride a bicycle on a winter day, and our little street, my clothes, the cobblestones, and the surrounding buildings are tinted steely blue. At four I fell in love with Mathieu, a boy of five who smiled at me and then stuck his hand in my turtle aquarium. My turtles, Mathieu's eyes, his sweater with sleeves pulled up past his elbows, live on in cool shades of green.

My fevers still seem red to me, and happy winter days steely blue. But I do not have other yellow memories, not even of the brightest summer afternoon. Yellow is the day my brother arrived from the children's home.

It might be the fear and jealousy I felt—my parents do not remember the day as having been particularly yellow—but the sunlight seemed blinding outside our long, French windows. We lived on a quai above the Seine in Paris, and the sun glinted so brightly on the river you could not look at it for long or without squinting.

My father stood on the balcony leaning on the railing with a Scotch and soda in his hand. I was restless. I did not have the patience to stand in one place for long, and ran to and from the balcony. Joining my father for the twentieth time, I pushed my head into his hip and tugged at his back pocket to get his attention. But he was not in the mood to pay attention to me.

"DADDY-Y-Y-Y. Is the little brother coming soon?"

"Any minute now," my father said, not looking at me. He was watching the taxis crossing the wide cement bridge.

"DADDY-Y-Y-Y. I changed my mind. Tell him not to come today."

"Will you behave yourself?" he said, annoyed. "I mean, you really do have to behave yourself. He's going to be scared to death."

"Jesus, Bill," my mother said from the other side of the long, cream-colored living room which was bathed in yellow light. She had gotten all dressed up in a pale Chanel suit with matching shoes and she could not sit still, like me. "You want to go to the park with Candida, Channe? Maybe she should go to the—"

"She's got to be here, Marcella," my father said in a completely calm voice. When he said something in that calm, even tone, no one had the courage to contradict him. I ran off toward the kitchen to bother my nurse for a glass of water. She had been told to stay in the kitchen so that the little brother would not be confused by too many strangers all at once. The waiting seemed interminable and everyone, including Candida, was tense and not in the mood to baby me.

"Here. Come here, Channe. Look," my father called from the balcony. I ran to him and stuck my face between two iron bars decorated with iron leaves. A taxi had stopped before the house. The door flew open and a heavy shoe stepped out and landed on the pavement. It was followed by a gray skirt and then a gray head. The woman looked around for a moment and leaned into the taxi and tugged at something still hidden in the car. A little bare leg appeared on the edge of the seat, then another. The woman pulled at one of the knees and a blond head popped out.

My father moved away from the window, removing my hand from his back pocket. Feeling completely abandoned I went, dragging my feet, over to the fireplace and hid beneath the jutting wooden mantle.

Forever, I thought. He was coming to live with us

forever and the thought was as confusing to me as the idea of the universe going on forever.

The little brother's story had been explained to me in careful detail. I was three when the decision to bring him had been made, and a year had passed since then. His natural parents had died in a car accident right after his birth. This was not true but I have never blamed my parents for withholding this information, as anything else would have been too much for my intellect and the little brother's as well.

He had spent his first three years with a French couple who had only fostered him, not adopted him, and when the foster mother had killed herself by taking sleeping pills, the father, unable to cope, had put the little boy in a children's home. The couple had been acquaintances of my parents. One day the man called my father and said, "Bill, remember that little boy your wife thought was so adorable? As I remember she said there was nothing in the world she wanted more than a boy like that—well, I can't keep him, Bill. He's in a children's home right now and I can't stand it."

But it was illegal for Americans to adopt French children, and my parents had bribed and pleaded and paid thousands and thousands of dollars to some official to have my brother's birth papers disappear. My mother had even had a private audience with Madame de Gaulle (my father's position as a celebrated American writer living in Paris opened up all sorts of influential doors) and she, the wife of the President of France, had pushed the whole thing through by writing a letter of recommendation. Even with Madame de Gaulle's recommendation, the deal was tenuous—I did not know this either until many years later: Once a month for the next several years a person from the social service agency came to check on us. One bad word from that person could have sent the little brother back to the children's home. My parents lived in terror from the moment the little brother walked in the door.

"No two people ever fought harder to have a kid in the world," my father had told me over and over again, during the year it took them to get through the bureaucracy.

"Didn't you fight hard to have me?"

"Yes, we sure did. But it was a different kind of fight. Your mommy was sick. She can't have any more babies and you always say you're so lonely. Now you'll have someone to play with all the time."

Someone to play with *all the time*! Someone to share *every*thing with, I thought. Someone who would be sleeping next door, in my old playroom!

I heard the doorbell ring and then some French being spoken. My parents spoke French badly, while I spoke almost fluently; I'd been such a terror they'd sent me off to school at the age of two. I heard my father ask the woman if she wanted a cup of tea or coffee or a cold drink. She said *non, merci* in a grave voice.

"Channe," my father called out in the calm voice that everyone listened to, "come here."

Out I came from under the fireplace mantle and there was the little brother. He stood as though frozen, his arms crossed over a small, battered black suitcase he kept pressed to his chest. He wore a plaid suit which must have fit him when he was two. My mother says it was blue, but I remember it was yellow with orange lines. The sleeves were too short and the shorts were stretched so that the front pockets bulged out. He would not look up from the floor. His knuckles were white from gripping the suitcase. He had a round head and juicy pink cheeks and a mouth like a young rosebud. Every now and then a sigh escaped from his nose and his nostrils flared.

The woman's head turned left and right, scrutinizing everything. She had purple wormlike blood vessels on her cheeks and a lipless mouth.

"*Présentez-vous*, Benoit," she said softly to the little brother, giving him a slight push at the shoulder. He tottered, but kept his ground and his arms around the suitcase.

"It's all right," my father said in a gentle voice. He got down on one knee in front of the little brother and put out his hand.

"*Je suis ton père*," he said in his awful American accent, making the little brother frown. I am your father, he said. He's not his father! I thought, outraged.

4

"*Et voici ton mère et ton soeur.*"

Ton *mère*! I thought, it's not ton *mère*, it's ta *mère*. I came forward, not too close, and said in French to the strange woman and the little brother, "Please forgive my father, he doesn't speak French very well, he's a foreigner."

"What does he have in the suitcase?" my mother asked the woman, trying to sound relaxed but her voice was too high, too enthusiastic.

"A pair of underwear, a pair of socks, and another shirt."

"Channe," my father said, stretching his arm out and encircling me conspiratorially. "Listen, sweetheart, do me a favor, will you? You know where the toys are we got for him. Will you bring the box up here? You can give them to him yourself."

"No," I said flatly.

The look my father gave me made me feel like the Wicked Witch of the West when the bucket of water is thrown at her.

"Excuse us a moment, please," he said, and nodded sideways toward the hallway that led down to the kitchen, the playroom, my room, and my nanny Candida's room. I knew I had to go or there would be *serious trouble* later on.

The old playroom had a red tile floor. My mother had brought in a little rug and a bed. I kicked the box with the new toys in it and it skidded across the floor and hit my father's feet. He kicked the box out of the way, lifted me up and sat me down on the little brother's new bed.

"I want you to pick up that box and take it down the hall and give it to him," he said calmly, slowly. "Right now. You are being awful and I'm embarrassed. Just look at that poor, terrified little boy and look at you. I'm horrified. He's scared to death of us. You're the only person his age around here. Maybe he'll talk to you. Can't you try to be nice?" He paused a moment, seeing that I was about to cry.

More gently, he said, "What if Mama and I were gone forever? Wouldn't you want someone to be nice to you?"

I began to heave deep sighs and my face contorted completely. I jumped off the bed and threw myself around his thighs.

"Daddy-y-y, Daddy-y-y, don't say that!"

"Please, baby. Please, for me, please go give him the box."

I dragged the box down the long hall to the living room. My father helped a little by pushing it along with his foot. I left it in front of the little brother indifferently, as though I were abandoning something worthless.

"*Tiens,*" I said. "*C'est pour toi.*"

"*P-pardon?*" he said.

"*C'EST POUR TOI!*"

"*Pour moi?*" He frowned, pointing a finger inward, toward his chest which was somewhere behind the suitcase. His eyes were round and blue and he had a little space between his front teeth.

"Open it," I said.

He pinned the suitcase up under his left arm and with his free hand opened the box.

"Put your suitcase down," I said. He shook his head.

"*MAIS POSE TA VALISE!*" I yelled.

My mother looked at my father and her mouth twitched.

"Darling, you're too abrupt. Please don't be so bossy," she suggested to me. "Bill, darling, say something." Tiny drops of sweat appeared above her eyebrows.

"Channe," my father said, clearing his throat, "don't be so bossy."

The little brother pulled the red fire engine out of the box and held it up with difficulty. "Oh, the pretty truck," he sighed. He looked toward the woman and then put the fire engine down on the carpet, resigned to giving it up.

"No, no, it's for you," my father insisted.

"They are not used to such expensive gifts, Madame," the woman said in a quiet, disapproving tone.

The little brother placed the suitcase flat on the carpet and sat on it, admiring the fire engine from a distance.

"But look, silly!" I said, becoming enthusiastic, "I won't take it from you, I just want to show you, see! It runs by itself and goes pin-pon-pin!" I turned it over and wound the key. The fire engine took off, a blaring yellow light flashing

6

on top. Yellow, yellow, yellow! the light flashed. The siren made a terrible racket and I was thrilled because toys weren't generally allowed in the living room.

The fire engine banged into an antique wooden chair at the other end of the room, turned around by itself, and headed back. It went straight to the little brother, as though it knew its rightful owner, and banged into the suitcase between his spread legs. He lifted it off the floor and hugged it as though it were a small dog. His face was so red it almost matched the truck.

"SEE! I told you. Pin-pon-pin!" I shouted.

He wound the toy, put it back on the floor and after a moment of deliberation, left his suitcase to chase it around the room. He started to laugh then, his face all red and his eyes round, and I started to laugh too because I had never seen anybody get so excited over a toy.

The woman said she was leaving then, and the little brother immediately abandoned the fire truck and headed toward the door, grabbing his suitcase on the way.

"*Non*, Benoit," she said, "you are staying here."

"B-by myself?" he asked in a shaky voice.

"You'll be very happy," she said, patting his shoulder lightly. My father shook hands with the woman at the door and then closed it behind her. Benoit stood before the door and stared at it for a long time with the suitcase pressed once again to his chest. His rose lips curved downward and his face went completely white. He looked bereft, in pain, aghast. I mustn't cry, his eyes said bravely, and I felt a pain I had never known before. I did not like myself at all and became furious at him for making me feel that way.

"Come on!" I said, pulling hard at his sleeve. "Let's play. See? There's another truck for you." I ran to the box and dug inside it.

"COME HERE! Look at this one, it carries rocks and dumps them all over the floor, all by itself."

I wound the truck and put my patent-leather shoes in the flatbed so that he could watch them being dumped on the floor. He took a few uncertain steps in my direction, but would not talk or play and continued to grip the suitcase.

* * *

My mother pulled together cookies and milk and ice cream in the kitchen while Candida followed her around, pointing to the right cabinets and drawers. The little brother ate up everything quickly, as though he thought my mother might change her mind and take it all away from him.

"Won't you put your suitcase down on the floor? Look, you can put it between your legs," she said in French.

He conceded, finally, and moved it from his lap to the floor. This was after my mother agreed to let him have a second bowl of ice cream. Half of the first bowl had ended up on the suitcase and I was disgusted because if *I* had behaved that way I wouldn't have been allowed to finish the *first* bowl.

We went from the kitchen to our rooms and the little brother almost fainted from shock at seeing my toys. I had twenty stuffed bears who lived on my bed whose names I changed every few days and five Barbie dolls with yellow hair who had their own beauty parlor and closet. They were spread out in different twisted positions, some undressed, some half-dressed, their tiny shoes scattered about like pieces of chewed gum. I also had a Lego set and was building a castle out of red, white, and blue bricks. There were half-constructed puzzles and coloring books everywhere.

The little brother stared but would not touch. He had his suitcase and his two trucks in his arms and these he would not part with. I naturally was bored with my own toys and wanted to play with his trucks and a tremendous fight erupted.

Candida dragged me off screaming to the kitchen, and my mother took the little brother out shopping for clothes in the neighborhood. In a moment of crisis (when I fell ill, for example) my mother's reaction was always to buy, buy, buy. I was not the victim of this crisis but the cause; suddenly my whole little world was standing on its head.

Candida was peeling potatoes and onions at the kitchen table, her large, chafed hands moving swiftly over a glass bowl. She had come from Portugal at twenty-five, without her family, and had been with us since I was two months old.

I spent more time with her than anyone else, watched her cook, sew, clean, shine our shoes, and these daily routines had a calming effect on me. "I am your second mommy," she would tell me in all seriousness. She was my ally, my best friend, but she was not my *protectrice* although she often tried to be—she was as terrified of my father's wrath as I was.

The kitchen was disturbingly quiet that afternoon. The radio was off and the bright light above our heads buzzed like a mosquito.

"I hate him," I told her. Candida sighed deeply but for once would not agree with me.

"He's ugly," I said. "He's dumb."

"Ay, ay, ay, Channa," she said. Candida added *as, os,* and *is* to the ends of words. "Don't talk like that."

"You don't love me anymore too," I said.

"Ay, ay, ay," she said, sighing.

The little brother spread his new clothes out on his bed, organizing by color. He put the new blue shorts with the blue pajamas, the red shirt with the red socks, and so on.

"That's not how you're supposed to do it," I said.

"Leave him alone," my mother said.

"*Pour moi, pour moi, et pour moi,*" he said, touching each thing admiringly with a flat hand.

He brought his suitcase out from beneath the bed and opened it. He put all the clothes in and zipped it shut and put it back under the bed.

"You have a closet of your own here." My mother pointed to the unvarnished wooden closet that had arrived yesterday.

"When I go, can I take the clothes and the trucks with me?" he asked her.

"You are going to stay with us forever," she said.

He looked at her with the same expression he'd worn when the strange woman had left him at the front door.

Every day was like a holiday that first week. I was out of school for the summer, but instead of sending me to the park or shopping for groceries with Candida, my father quit work at lunchtime and took the family out. We went rowing on the Marne, picnicking in the country, out to fancy restaurants, and walking for hours around the Latin Quarter. He took us to the Lido Club on the Champs Élysées to eat hamburgers. The little brother ate four hamburgers with fried onions (since he was allowed to so was I, but I could not finish my third) and then we went to the movies. We saw lots of cowboy movies in English and my father told the little brother about America.

"Ben-wa," my father called the little brother. We only spoke to him in American now, except when we were with Candida.

"Ben-wa sounds terrible in English," my father said one day. We were having lunch in the Brasserie Lipp and the little brother and I were eating escargots, pulling them out of the shells with a tiny fork and sopping the baguette in the rich butter sauce.

"Maybe we should change it?" he suggested.

"But to what?" my mother said.

"I don't know. Let him decide."

"He's too little to decide his own name," I said.

"No he's not," my mother said. She had this childish sing-song tone in her voice sometimes, "Goody-goody gumdrops," she called it; I hated it, and was convinced she was using it right then to inflame my already inflamed being.

"Then I want to change my name, too," I said with a mouth full of bread and sauce.

"No," my father said flatly.

"I won't answer unless you call me Jenny from now on," I said.

"I'll call you Agatha, how's that?" my mother said in that same voice.

My mother's father had died when she was sixteen and I think she never lost her childhood. She was never given the opportunity to rebel against her strong father. She acted like a child with me, but the only time I ever saw her cry was when she'd describe her father, a strong-willed, handsome, blue-eyed Italian man. Sometimes she would wail like a baby and put her head down between her arms. Sometimes, in that childish voice, she would say, "My daddy was as nice as your daddy."

"Agatha," my mother said as I sopped up the last of the escargot sauce, "would you like some dessert?"

"You're Agatha," I said.

"Cut it out, you two," my father said. "Ben-wa, would you like a new name?" He said this in American, slowly, several times, and then in French.

The little brother shrugged indifferently. You could never tell what he was thinking or if he even understood what was going on around him, and that drove me crazy too.

"Think about it," my father said. "You don't have to do anything you don't want to do."

After about five days he moved his clothes from the suitcase to the closet, but kept the suitcase under the bed.

It was that night, I think, that I was awakened by terrible whimpering sounds coming through the open archway that connected our two rooms. I got up and went to his bed in my bare feet. His tile floor was cold and I sat down on his bed and tucked my feet up under my nightgown.

"What is it?" I whispered.

"*Le loup-garou*," he said.

"What *loup-garou*?" *Loup-garou* was the French were-wolf.

"He's here."

"No he's not."

"I did pipi. They're going to beat me." He slid a hand out from under the covers and reached under the bed, his hand groping blindly in the dark space.

"Don't worry, it's still there," I said as though he were the stupidest person in the world. "And they're not going to beat you. I promise you nobody's going to beat you."

"You can draw already and you can write your own name," he said in a dismal voice.

"Didn't they teach you to draw and write There?"

He thought about this in silence for a minute. "Yes," he said finally, "but I couldn't't."

11

"Tomorrow we'll ask papa to show you how to write your own name. What was it like, There?" I asked.

"It was all right," he said in that indifferent tone.

"Did you have lots of friends?"

"Everyone was all right except Sister Elene. She used to beat us for doing pipi in bed."

"Where did you get that suitcase?"

"I don't remember. Leave me alone." He dug his head into the pillow.

"Take off your pajama if it's wet. Here, I'll get you another one." I went to the wall and switched on the light. I opened his closet drawer and took out another brand-new pair of pajama pants which he had folded neatly, and placed according to color, next to some socks.

"Here," I handed them to him. He changed quickly, under the sheets. His feet and knees kicked the sheets up in all directions. I put the wet pants on the floor in the corner and switched off the light.

"*NON!* Don't turn off the light. The *loup-garou* comes in the dark. Sister Elene says he only eats bad children."

"*You're* not bad. You're as good as can be. I'm much badder than you, and no *loup-garou* is going to get me."

He thought about this for a while, frowning in that stubborn way. He did not seem convinced.

"Anyway papa would shoot any *loup-garou* that tried to get in our house. You want to come sleep with me? You can sleep with me if your bed is wet."

"All right," he said, throwing back the covers. He crouched down and brought his suitcase out from beneath the bed.

"You're not going to bring that stupid old thing, too, are you? Nobody's going to take it."

"I'll just put it down beside your bed. All right?"

It was strange to have him in my bed. I had a girlfriend who lived next door who slept over sometimes. We would talk and talk until we fell asleep. I didn't know what to talk about with Benoit. It wasn't as though he'd be gone tomorrow and everything had to be said right now.

"Well, then. Good night," he said.

"Good night."

I lay awake for a while, listening to his deep and even breathing and watching his round face, his heavy eyelids, his puffy mouth, finally at peace and comfortable in sleep. I hoped his dreams were good ones. I hoped that tomorrow I would be able to be nice. When we fought and my parents were not around, Candida took my side and smacked him or sent him to play in his room. Afterward I would watch him, feeling vindicated and righteous, through the crack in his door. He would sit on the floor hunched over his trucks and hum melancholy tunes he made up as he went along. I adored Candida for favoring me, but I knew it was not right. The strangest thing about it was that Benoit never told on us. My parents had no idea.

Why was it so hard to be nice all the time? Wasn't it easier to be nice? Why, on the rare occasion that I *was* nice, did I suddenly feel so rotten about all the times I wasn't nice to him? Why did he always make me want to pull his hair or bite him ferociously? Either that or he gave me a feeling of utter self-disgust, emptiness, and gloom. I wished there was a place they could send me to teach me to be nice. Like the place where he had been. I only wished this for a second, because I knew it was a place where there was no Candida, no parents, and no one to protect me.

For lunch on Saturday we went to the brasserie at the end of the island on which we lived, to celebrate that Benoit had been with us a week. It had been the longest week of my life and I did not think there was anything to celebrate at all, especially if the coming weeks were going to be as long as that one.

Benoit had two slices of *tarte aux framboises* for dessert and my father brought up the subject of changing his name again.

"*J' sais pas,*" the little brother said. He had pieces of raspberry all over his face, even high on his cheeks, and I was disgusted.

"Bill," my mother said, "why don't we give him a name. How about Anthony, like my father?"

"I *told* you he's too little to pick his own name. Look, he's got sticky stuff all over the place."

13

"Be quiet, Agatha," my mother said.

"Let's give it a little while," my father said. "Let him think about it."

After the brasserie, I liked to hold my father's hand and run along the top of the four-foot-high cement rampart that ran all along the upper quai. It gave me the feeling I could fly. Below, on the lower quai, were dogs and fishermen and the murky river splashed loudly against the embankment.

"Daddy! On the wall! On the wall!" I reached up to him. My father lifted me onto the rampart and gripped my wrist. I skipped and yelled as I ran along the two-foot-wide wall, arms spread out and flailing the air.

"MORE! MORE!" I shouted, but my father lifted me off and put me down on the sidewalk.

"Ben-wa, do you want to walk on the wall?"

"*Non.*"

"He's such a scaredy-cat he'll never do it," I said.

"Look, I'll lift you up and you can see how you feel about it." My father only spoke to the little brother in American now, and he seemed to understand the gist of things well enough although he would only respond in French.

He lifted Benoit onto the rampart and Benoit started to scream. Tears poured from his wide-open eyes.

"*NON! NON!*" he cried. He threw his arms around my father's neck and crawled onto him, his feet scrambling to hook onto something at my father's waist.

"It's all right. It's all right," my father kept saying.

"*Papa, non, j'veux pas! J'veux pas!*"

"I told you he's scared," I said. This didn't make me feel better at all, though I had hoped it would. I felt sick inside from his fear and grabbed my mother's hand. She squeezed it tightly.

"I'm sorry, Mommy."

"It's not your fault."

My father's hand held the back of the little brother's neck while he rocked him from side to side. Benoit pressed his face into my father's chest.

"O, papa," he said. "O, papa papa papa. I'll walk on the wall. You'll see, I can do it."

"We'll try it some other day," my father said, walking toward our house with the little brother in his arms. "O, papa papa," Benoit kept saying, as though it were the only word he could remember.

My father went upstairs to his office and wrote every day but Sunday. It was the only day of the week he slept late. It was also Candida's day off and my mother had to go to the kitchen to pour the water into the coffee pot that Candida had left out on a tray with the cups and sugar the night before. Then we had a ritual. My mother called to me and I ran to the kitchen and went downstairs with her to their room which was below the living room. I crawled onto the enormous bed and had a glass of milk in a coffee cup while they had their coffee and discussed our plans for the day.

This was Benoit's second Sunday. When my mother called from the kitchen I stopped by Benoit's room on my way.

"It's Sunday. Are you coming?"

"Not right away," he said. He was organizing his suitcase again. It was lying open on his bed and he was taking things out and putting things in. I didn't wait to see what and ran down the hall, happy to have my parents to myself for a few minutes.

My mother's voice always sounded gravelly on Sunday mornings. She was slow to wake up and her eyes seemed puffier than on other days.

"Where's your brother?"

"Doing something in his room."

"There's a John Wayne cowboy movie on TV at two," my father said. "We'll go have Vietnamese and then watch the movie. Maybe I'll put on my cowboy hat and boots. Maybe I'll get my pistols out too." My father had a real cowboy outfit he'd bought in the west when he was young; he liked to put it on when "humdinger" cowboy movies were on TV. He had gotten Benoit a toy cowboy hat and a gun belt, a special belt for bullets, two big black pistols and a little cowboy vest with fringes. Now they'll probably both get dressed up together from now on, I thought, wanting a cowboy suit.

We heard Benoit's footsteps coming down the stairs. Something thumped loudly on the stairs behind him.

He came in carrying the suitcase. He hopped up onto my father's side of the bed and crawled toward him with the suitcase dragging beside him. He put it down on my father's lap, over the sheet, and said, "*C'est pour vous.*"

"For me?" my father said.

"*Pour vous.*"

"Are you sure? My God, Ben-wa, that's the nicest present I've ever gotten in my life." My father unzipped the little suitcase and peered inside. In it was everything the little brother had arrived with, including the plaid suit he had been wearing.

In French, the little brother said, "I want to call myself little Bill."

"Little Bill? Billy. All right." My father's voice went quiet.

"Billy Anthony Willis," my mother said. "How's that, everybody? All right?"

"Billy," the little brother said.

"Isn't that something? I've hated my name all my life and he wants my name."

"Billy! Billy!" I said, jumping up and down on the bed. The cups jiggled on their saucers, my mother grabbed the tray and steadied it. She did not reprimand me.

"I just have this feeling," she said in her gravelly voice, "I really had no idea but now I think everything's going to be all right."

I see the rich velvety colors of the curtains and bedspread and the antique bedside lamps bathing us in amber light. I see the little brother's flushed and smiling face, his sweet blue eyes all watery and the dark space glinting between his front teeth.

We had our first four-way kiss. The little brother put one arm around my father's neck and one around my mother's. I was on the other side. Our four mouths came together in a loud smack.

The happiness I felt did not last through the day, nor did

it return the next day, but at the moment of the four-way kiss I was happy that he was mine and that I was his. For a short moment I was almost in love with him, for he was certainly brave, much more so than I would ever be, and had somehow found it possible to forgive me.

A SOLDIER'S DAUGHTER
NEVER CRIES

I sat down at the top of the metro steps in the pouring rain, cringing as sudden blasts of wind slapped the rain against my face. The ground rumbled beneath me. It was the next train pulling in. I heard its doors slide open, and thirty seconds later a crowd of cranky French people came rushing up the stairs. It was just past five o'clock and everyone wanted to get home as fast as possible except me. The French people pushed and shoved and grumbled aloud, *"Quel sale temps de chien."*

I watched a man in a suit push a woman out of the way as he climbed the stairs. The woman yelled, *"Ah, ça, alors! Merde!"* and swung her handbag, hitting the man across the face. He turned back and called her a *putain.* He ran on up toward me and stepped on my gray uniform skirt, smearing mud all over the pleats.

"And what the hell are you doing sitting there!" he shouted. "You want to catch the *grippe?*"

I refused to look up. Instead, I tried to wipe the mud off my skirt. One after another, four more trains rumbled in. One fat woman's high heel speared my shoe at the instep, grazing the skin. The scratch stung pretty badly, but would not bleed in a dramatic way at all.

I felt terribly sorry for myself and wanted to fall ill or have an accident before I reached home. I'd had pneumonia once, three years before, and I remembered in the red haze of my fever that the entire household had come to a standstill. My father had held my hand while I lay facedown on my parents' bed and the doctor gave me a shot in the behind. My father said in a gentle voice that if I relaxed my muscles the shot wouldn't hurt and he'd been right. I had been so sick that he'd even given up work for one whole day to watch over me personally.

What I needed now was to come down with a serious high fever like that one, before I had to face my father.

I picked up my *cartable*, heavy with exercise books, and stood. I wiped the itchy gravelly dirt off the backs of my legs and opened my navy-blue blazer. At the curb I stood in the gutter while I waited for the light. The water had a current in it and was ice-cold and I wiggled my toes inside the blue loafers. I sneezed three times, a good sign.

Madame Beauvier, the *directrice,* had called me down to her office in the middle of class. In the middle of class! The teacher and all of my classmates had turned in silence and stared at me as I left the room. I felt all their eyes on my back as I went through the door; it sent a shiver up my spine.

I knew exactly why I was being sent down to Madame Beauvier and fear forced me to grip the banister as I descended the wide, vinyl-covered stairs. They would probably expel me for what I'd done. There was no feeling left in my knees. I had never been in trouble before and had always gotten on perfectly politely with Madame Beauvier. But Madame Beauvier's anger terrified everybody because it was so calm and expressed itself in such odd ways. Once, I'd seen her take an enormous pair of scissors out of her pocket and snip off a loudmouth's bangs, right in the middle of the crowded hallway. "I told you last week, Antoine, to get a hair-cut," Madame Beauvier said. She had not raised her high voice or even frowned.

Madame Beauvier was waiting for me behind her tall desk. She was a short woman with small, hunched shoulders and a tight, pale face. She had the longest and most beautiful bright red nails I had ever seen. They were so long she used the eraser end of a pencil to dial the phone.

"Bonjour, Mademoiselle Charlotte-Anne!" she said en-

ergetically in a voice that sounded like a violin off key, as though she were thrilled to see me, who stood paralyzed two feet from the desk.

Oh boy, I thought, this is it. No one called me by my full name anymore: Charlotte-Anne, I'd learned on my first day of kindergarten, sounded in French almost exactly like "charlatan". It was a word I'd never heard before that day, but it suddenly appeared everywhere—in poems, songs; and even teachers could not resist making a little joke about it.

I asked them to write Channe, my nickname at home, on everything, even my report cards. At first they'd refused, claiming that it was improper and against the rules, but my father backed me up. He called Madame Beauvier and told her that if they would not write my name the way I wanted it written, he supposed he'd just have to find me another school that would. Then he threatened to send me to their rival, the American Middle School, which he never would have done because the Middle School, in his opinion, was much too narrow-mindedly American.

Madame Beauvier leaned forward and crossed her long, delicate fingers on the desk top.

"Tell me, Mademoiselle Charlotte-Anne," she said in French in a confidential tone, "how do you spell gymnastics?"

I stared at Madame Beauvier's hands and did not respond. The hands slid below the desk top and opened a drawer, withdrawing a little folded paper from it. They carefully unfolded the paper and spread it out flat on the desk.

"This is your excuse from gymnastics class . . ." She waited a bit. "Your father is a successful American writer, is he not? Your father, it seems to me, would know how to spell gym? Yet," she slid the paper toward me with the tips of the nails, turning it around. "Here gym is spelled J-I-M. This is your father's signature, is it not?"

"No," I mumbled. "I did it, Madame. I didn't feel well."

"We have an infirmary." Her voice went terribly high then, but remained calm. "I have telephoned your father. Normally, you would be expelled for this." She picked up

20

one of her fresh yellow pencils and tapped its eraser against the desk top. I thought, I'm going to have to run away from home.

"Considering you have never been in trouble with us before, and that you are not a terrible student and have been with us since the *jardin d'enfants*—four years, isn't it? We have decided to give you a chance. We have left it up to your parents to punish you as they see fit."

Tears fell from my eyes, but I refused to grimace. I stood frozen before Madame Beauvier, who was slowly shaking her head.

"I'm sorry," she said simply. "Go back to your class and finish the day."

The rain stopped as I was crossing the bridge to the Île Saint-Louis. I was not nearly cold or wet enough. My father would not feel sorry for me. I stood in a puddle at the end of the bridge and stared down at my reflection. The white blouse wriggled into the blue blazer and gray skirt. Would he beat me? He had never beaten me, although he sometimes threatened, making a fist and shaking it in the air, "I'm going to beat you to a pulp!"

Maybe I could tell him I'd been hit by a car. He would not believe me. Where could I go? With a sense of utter doom, I crossed the quai and headed down Rue des Deux Ponts toward my house.

I tiptoed up the back stairwell, past the first floor, because my nanny would be waiting for me there and she'd have made me change my clothes before going to him. I climbed the three creaking, splintered flights of stairs in the dark. The *cartable* thumped quietly on every step as I dragged it up by the strap.

My father spent every day up in his study, away from the rest of the house, writing long, important books. There had been two already, before I was born. Now he was writing Number Four. It had to be terribly important, because no one was allowed up in his office except for emergencies. Once when Billy and I had been cleaning the fishbowl, one of the fish went down the sink. Billy flew up the three flights to the office screaming, "DADDY! DADDY! THE FISH!

CHANNE! THE FISH!" And our father had come charging down the stairs like a lightning bolt. He'd thought I'd swallowed a fish bone. With tweezers he pulled the fish out of the drain and saved its life. Now it had a tear in its tail and was our favorite. I wished that this emergency were more like the one with the fish.

I tapped softly on the office door with my knuckles. I waited a few minutes and he did not come. I turned away and felt for the stairs, sliding my foot in the dark. Maybe, I thought, I could have an accident by falling down the stairs? But the deep black stairwell frightened me. I was going to get it one way or the other, no matter what, and my father, I decided, would certainly not kill me although falling down the stairs might. Turning back, I kicked the door with the toe of my shoe. I heard his footsteps and then I heard my heart pounding in my head. He opened the door. The smell of his office wafted out from behind him; all his odors seemed to conglomerate here into one strong, alien, and not very fatherly smell. I recognized pipe smoke, old black coffee, fresh shaving soap and aftershave, the light metallic grease of his exercise and office machines, and his strange, acrid sweat.

"Hello, you," he said in a gruff voice. I looked up and saw deep wrinkles in his forehead. His eyebrows came together over his nose so that they looked like one curly salt-and-pepper moustache. He had a chin that stuck out like Popeye's, which usually made me smile, but today his lips were pressed into one thin angry line.

"Come on in here and sit down. We have to have a serious talk."

I couldn't move. "Come on," he said, "take off your jacket and sit." He walked away from the door. My face was burning up and I could not look up from the floor.

"You're all wet. Take off your shoes." He turned back and put his hand on my shoulder, leading me toward the radiator below the window. He crouched before me, tugged at my shoes and placed them on the windowsill. I lifted my skirt and spread it out in a circle around me as I sat down. The chair came from the Village Suisse and was an antique with a peach-colored velvet seat. He cleared his throat.

"Madame Beauvier called me today."

"I know," I mumbled. "She told me when I was in her office."

"You did a very bad thing, you know." I looked at my feet. I was trying to squeeze them between the radiator tubes. The heat stung fiercely.

"Were you by yourself? Was it your idea to forge my signature?"

"It was me and Melissa," I mumbled. "We both did it. We didn't feel like going to gym today 'cause it was raining."

"That's no reason to forge my signature. You know, if you were older you could go to jail for that. It's a very serious crime to sign someone else's name. It's against the law." My father did not raise his voice; he maintained a stern, even tone. His eyes, when I glanced at them quickly, seemed worried rather than angry.

I wished he would yell or give me that licking he was always talking about. Then I could be furious at him. If he'd slap me I'd cry, then we'd make up and love each other again and forget it. But he wasn't mad, he was disappointed, and that was horrible.

"You're just too damn used to getting what you want. I guess I've been too easy on you." He sighed, then, as he did whenever he was trying to think hard, and pressed his hand against his wrinkled forehead and rubbed his eyebrows. When he did this his eyes focused on nothing and he became cross-eyed.

I began to cry. I clenched my teeth and pressed my lips together. I thought of his hugs and kisses when I fell and hurt myself, when he bandaged my sprains and cuts and whispered our secret to me—a soldier's daughter never cries.

He stood by the tall window and looked out at the dismal day. The building across the street was old and gray, darker than the sky. I watched him arch his back and bring his shoulder blades and elbows together behind him.

"I'm sore," he said. "I've been sitting up here all day. That goddamn Beauvier's voice sends chills down my back that make my hairs stand up. It's stopped raining. You dry enough?" He turned to me. I nodded.

"Want to go for a walk?"

I nodded again. He bent over me and helped me with the jacket and shoes. "Shoes are still damp," he said, sliding them onto my feet.

"It's not cold out," I said.

Just then the phone buzzed. It was the recently installed line that connected my father's office to the rest of the house.

"Hello," he said. There was a pause. "She's here, honey. Everything's okay. We're going for a walk . . . I'm explaining," he said in a preoccupied tone. "She's very sorry." He told my mother we'd be back in an hour or so and hung up.

"Here." He took an olive cashmere sweater off the back of his office chair and wrapped it around my shoulders like a shawl. It was the same color as his eyes.

"I don't want to stop downstairs and involve the whole damn house in this."

I was immensely relieved that he wasn't planning to force me to atone in front of the entire family.

We went down to the riverbank. The lower quai ran almost completely around our side of the island, the southern side. It was where people walked their dogs, and lovers sat on the green park benches and "necked." I had learned this word from him and did not quite know what it meant although I knew it involved boys and girls and sounded dirty.

Once we rounded the first bend, Notre Dame was in full view, looming tall and gray across the river.

"You know, I like the pissy smell this place has," my father said.

"Oo, gross, Daddy."

He took slow, even steps so that I could keep up with him. After a while he held my hand. My mother and Candida seemed to forget when my brother and I were holding on and made us run to keep up. My father never seemed to be in any hurry. I watched the cobblestones and tried to avoid the cracks because it was good luck.

He said, after a long silence, "I don't know what to tell

you. You know I have to punish you. What do you think would be a fair punishment?"

"I don't know." I shrugged. "Maybe nobody can sleep over for a month?" I looked up at him and my eyes felt heavy. He nodded slowly but did not respond. He rubbed his forehead with his fingertips and squinted.

"Do you think that's reasonable, under the circumstances?"

"No desserts for a month, too?"

"Let me think about it," he said solemnly. I squeezed his large, dry hand. I could not tell if he felt it or not. There was a free bench a little further on and we sat down. I began to swing my legs back and forth beneath it.

"When I was younger," my father said, "before I met your mama, something like this happened to me. There was a guy in New York City called Bill Willis, like me. And he went around signing my name on bills in all sorts of places. Bars and restaurants and a few stores. He even took a lot of money out of my bank account. Over ten thousand dollars, that was an awful lot of money back then."

"Did you know him?"

"No."

"Did the police catch him?" I stopped swinging my legs and looked sideways at my father.

"Yeah, finally. But he'd spent all the money already." He was looking off toward Notre Dame.

I watched a bottle bob up and down in the greenish water, until the current carried it away under the bridge.

"Did you meet him, Daddy?"

"No. I never did. I didn't want to, really."

"But they made him pay you the money, didn't they?"

"How could they? He didn't have any to give."

"So he went to prison?"

"No, I let him go. I didn't press charges."

"But why?"

"I don't know, baby. I felt sorry for him, I guess."

"He should've gone to prison," I said with finality.

"But what if he had a wife and kids? What if they were hungry? Who knows . . ."

I frowned. "Oh," he sighed, "I don't know." He rubbed

the top of my head lightly with the tips of his fingers. I had thick, curly, dirty-blond hair like his. We both hated for people to touch our hair. I envied him because he was a grown-up and nobody chased him, brandishing a brush. Everyone said I looked like I had a rat's nest on my head. Sometimes I minded when my father absently passed his fingers through my hair, but today I did not.

"You're so nice, Daddy," I said. I pressed myself against his shoulder. He chuckled and I felt his chest shake.

"I'm too nice, that's my problem." He put an arm around me and I began to cry again.

"I'm sorry, Daddy," I sobbed. The world sank behind a curtain of tears. "Daddy, Daddy I'm sorry I'll never do it again I promise."

"Ssh, now. What'd I used to tell you? Remember?"

"A soldier's daughter never cries," I said.

"That's right. . . . Are you hungry?"

I shook my head.

"Well, I am, and since I'm the boss, I say let's go down to the brasserie and have us something to eat."

He sat me on a barstool in front of the pinball machine and slipped two francs into the slot. "You're getting pretty good at this," he said, standing behind me with a hand on my shoulder. "Pretty soon you'll be beating your old man."

"Oh, no." I was concentrating on the ball.

The bar area was filled with workers who were stopping in for a drink on their way home. Most of them lived on the island and knew my father. They discussed their different jobs and the weather and the government with him. They liked him, I thought, because they considered him their own, personal American. And because his kids spoke French without accents and played in the street with their kids.

He showed me a new trick: how to capture the ball with the flipper and hold it so that I could aim my shot. Finally he lifted me off the stool.

"Time to go," he said.

As we walked along the upper quai, under the streetlights which were surrounded by yellow halos in the mist, he said, "I think you were being a little hard on yourself about your punishment. We'll just say no desserts for a month, how's that?"

I nodded slowly.

"And you'll give me your word you won't sneak into any bakeries on your way home from school?"

"I promise. I won't even look in the window. I won't see Melissa either."

He sighed and made a large circle with his arm, shoving the whole thing away from him. "You don't have to do that."

When we reached the corner on which we lived, I tugged on his arm.

"Are you still mad at me, Daddy? Are you still sad?"

"No," he said. He looked straight into my face for a moment and then burst into a loud laugh.

"What's so funny?" I didn't think any of it was funny and was perplexed and slightly annoyed.

"You're in third grade and you still can't spell gym! How do you spell gym?"

"J . . . no, G-Y-M." I had difficulties with J and G because in French J was pronounced gee and G was pronounced jay. My father roared with laughter.

"I bet you'll remember now," he said.

Still laughing, he picked me up, sat me on his hip, and carried me into the house.

THE HOUSE
IN THE TREE

One summer, my parents rented a house outside Deauville with their friends the Smiths. The Smiths had three impossible daughters. Cassandra, the oldest, was fourteen. She considered herself too grown-up to care about our silly games and spent most afternoons, after the beach, trying on grown-up clothes: stockings of all colors and little pink and powder-blue garters and bras, which her mother bought her in the town's fancy boutiques. She might have been fun if she had been willing to let us gaze at her spoils, but no. Only the other two Smiths, Mary-Ellen and Gillis, were allowed in Cassandra's room. (Billy and I peeked anyway.) At first Billy and I had hoped to make an ally of Gillis as she was only ten, a year older than we. But Gillis was treated like a Princess Child by her older sisters and soon tired of our form of democracy, which was basically that she could not always have her way.

Their nanny Bethany did not speak French and our nanny Candida did not speak English, but those two got along just fine until a fight between the camps erupted. The fights usually started when the Smith girls accused Billy and me of not being really American. We were being raised in France, and could not, for example, tell the difference between quarters, dimes, and nickels. We had never eaten at a McDonald's or been to a drive-in movie. The Smith girls

28

wore embroidered peace signs on their bluejeans and knew all the words to the most recent, most popular anti-war rock 'n' roll songs. "Peace, brother," they would say, making the sign, or "The Black Panthers live," making the fist. The Vietnam War had not started to affect our Parisian lives yet; they considered us highly uninformed but would not teach us anything and took every opportunity to tell us what idiots we were. Billy and I spoke American with a strange close-mouthed lilt, putting emphasis on the wrong ends of phrases and mispronouncing words.

"It's not he *say-z*," one of them would invariably correct. "It's he *sez*. Can't you hear the *dif*ference? God, are you two Frogs."

This drove my brother to madness.

It had been five years since Billy had come to our house from the children's home. When he'd arrived he could not speak a word of English but had picked it up in a matter of months. The children we played with on our street in Paris called him Amerloque, a serious insult that Billy took as the highest of compliments. Telling him that he was not really American was about the worst insult anyone could lay on him. There were certain things I was forbidden to say to him (you are not really American being one) but the Smith girls did not have these rules; they probably did not even know Billy was adopted.

Until that summer, things between Billy and me had not improved much. I have to admit that I was far from being a good child. I was bossy, loud-mouthed, insecure, neurotic, and furiously jealous of my brother. Billy brought out the worst in me. But since the Smith girls picked on him as much as me, that particular summer we found solace in sticking together, sticking up for each other. For the first time since his arrival, I was happy for long stretches that Billy was my brother.

The parents were not around much. The reason we were there with the Smiths was that our father and Mr. Smith were writing a screenplay together "which could mean a lot of money," our father explained. Our mother and Mrs. Smith went to the racetrack at Clairefontaine practically every day and all four of them went to the casino in

Deauville at night. After our nannies brought us home from the beach we were given hours of free time to roam the property and invent games. The only iron rule was that we weren't to disturb the writers at work. Their presence in an upstairs room of the house hung over our activities like the eyes of God.

The house looked more like a château than a villa; it was a long, two-story stone edifice with a high slate roof and arching windows with little balconies. On the ground floor you could walk out onto the gravel terrace and the rose gardens through the tall windows of any room. Around the entire house went the white pebbled driveway, and around the driveway were enormous pink and pale-blue hydrangea bushes and white rhododendrons. There was a long, sloping green lawn where several ancient, magnificent oaks grew, and beyond the lawn was the untamed, deep green forest.

The Smith girls' favorite game was croquet. They would dress up and pretend they were duchesses parading on the lawn. Haw haw haw, they would laugh in a throaty way, as though whatever was funny was really not funny at all. It seemed to Billy and me that the two oldest girls were just as unpleasant to each other as they were to us, but with them it seemed to be some kind of inside joke and they never really became offended by one another.

Billy and I took to the woods, not so much because we loved the woods, but because it was the one place we were certain not to encounter the Smiths. "The woods are barbaric," Cassandra often said.

In the middle of the forest was a green chicken-wire fence that you couldn't see until you were right up against it. Behind the fence the trees and brambles went on out of sight. We decided that this must be where our property ended and the neighbors' began.

Billy and I invented all sorts of games, our favorites being Thierry la Fronde Saves The Fair Maiden From Certain Death At The Hands Of The Forest Elves, and The Heroic Cowboy Finds An Indian Squaw Tied To A Tree In The Woods Dying Of Hunger And Thirst. It always ended up with And They Get Married And Build A House In The Forest. That part wasn't much of a denouement because, after all,

Billy was my brother and we never even kissed. Sometimes we looked for the doors to Elves' houses in the thick roots of the large trees and at the bases of the big, flat brown mushrooms. This grew disappointing after a while, because the doors were too well hidden and although we called to the Elves and promised them no harm, they would not come out to play.

One afternoon, I stood with my back to a big tree, arms encircling the trunk behind me (I would not let Billy really tie me up, I didn't trust him that much). The woods were so dense and green that the sun-filled sky hardly made it through to the ground. There was the rustle of the leaves disturbing the fine ribbons of light around me, and then a face, pale, greenish, with a disheveled shock of dirty-blond hair, was suddenly staring at me, its dirty hands gripping the diamonds in the chicken wire.

"AAHHHH!" I screamed, and started to run in the direction Billy had gone.

"N'as pas peur!" a boy's voice called out. "Don't be afraid! I live here."

Billy came charging out of the brambles just ahead of me, and I stopped running.

"Salut!" the boy said. Billy gazed at him with his suspicious and impenetrable blue eyes.

"Salut," Billy said through a closed mouth. He had a long stick in his hand and was whacking at the underbrush.

"I live here." The head turned to the side and gestured over the shoulder. "Where are you from?"

"From Paris," Billy said. "But we're Americans."

"Americans! I don't believe you. How come you speak French then?"

"I told you we live in Paris."

"Want to see my tree house?" the boy said. "My father helped me build it."

"There's a fence," Billy said, still suspicious. He did not take to people easily.

"There's a hole a little ways down," the boy said, beginning to walk to the left, slowly, along the fence. Billy and I followed on our side. The boy's dirty fingers skidded along the diamonds as he went.

"My name's Stephane," he offered.

"I'm Channe. This is my brother Billy."

"You have strange names."

"That's 'cause we're American," Billy said with a certain amount of pride.

"What's it like, there?"

"Big," Billy said. "All the cars are big, the streets are big, the buildings are huge, and the people are bigger than French people."

"You make me laugh," the boy said derisively.

"It's true," I said. "The cars are as long as three French cars."

"Here's the hole in the fence," the boy said. He ran his fingers down the fence and pulled up on the bottom part of it.

"Maybe the Elves made a hole," I said.

"They don't exist," the boy said.

Once we were on his side he seemed big, much bigger than we, in any case. He was at least a head taller than Billy and had spots of dirt on his face and on his arms, up to the elbows. He was wearing a brownish shirt that faded into the background.

"I know these woods better than anyone except my father," he said. "My father is the caretaker of the big house over there."

"Show us your tree house," Billy said. The boy set off, turning his back and waving for us to follow.

But first Billy did something I found extraordinary; he very nonchalantly took a red handkerchief out of his pocket and tied it to the fence above the hole. What a Boy Scout! I thought. All our cousins back in Pennsylvania were Boy Scouts and Cub Scouts, and I bet they wouldn't have thought of doing that. I'll have to tell Daddy about how Billy remembers everything he tells us about playing in the woods, I thought. I was so overwhelmed with pride and affection that my heart began to pound in my head, making me dizzy.

"I think you're the best," I said to Billy, squeezing his arm as we followed the bigger boy through the brambles and thickets. Billy shrugged me off, blushing. He did not like compliments, never had, not since I'd known him.

The tree house was a beauty. It had a thick wooden floor propped at the fork of the largest branches, three walls, the back one with a large window, and an A-shaped roof. There was a ladder leading up to it which the boy climbed like a monkey. He sat in the house and gestured for us to follow.

"You go first," Billy said quietly, "in case you fall I'll be able to maybe catch you."

Normally I would have been angry at him for suggesting such a thing, but under the circumstances I considered him gentlemanly, and went first. I was wearing long cut-off shorts (a rarity, I always wore skirts, even in the woods) and thought that this was a good thing because he could not look up my skirt at my underwear.

The boy had a flashlight, some dirty pillows, a dirty blanket, a pack of Gauloises, a box of matches, a slingshot, a pile of stones, and a pocketknife in his tree house.

"I can kill squirrels from here with my slingshot," he said. "Just like Thierry la Fronde."

"Thierry la Fronde kills bad guys, not squirrels," I said, horrified.

"Here, watch," Stephane said. He sat over the edge of the open side of the tree house and aimed his slingshot at an adjoining tree. I could see movements in the leaves, birds and squirrels hopping about out of sight, making chirping sounds. He pulled back on the elastic thongs, pinching a large stone in the leather pad. His lips pulled back, exposing two rows of dangerous-looking teeth. Billy looked on in mute fascination.

"*NON! NON!* Don't do it, please!" I cried out and hid my face in my hands.

I heard the soft *pock* of the stone hitting wood. He'd missed! But a second later he had another stone aimed at the tree. I started to cry.

"Don't," my brother said in a quiet, determined voice. "You're upsetting my sister."

I couldn't believe what I'd heard. I wanted to throw my arms around his neck and kiss his juicy red cheek.

"We'd better go home, anyway," Billy said. "It's getting late."

"Well I'm staying here," Stephane said. "Go ahead and find your way by yourself." He let out a strange laugh. "You won't! You'll be lost for hours in the dark."

"I don't think so," Billy said in his equable voice. "You follow me," he said, setting out down the ladder. Just as his head disappeared Stephane gripped my wrist in his hard fingers.

"I like you," he whispered, and kissed me on the corner of the mouth. "You're so pretty." I was not able to speak or push him away. My heart was beating too fast and confusing thoughts raced through my head. His stranger's breath felt sweet on my face, his lips were soft as they touched mine so delicately. As soon as he relaxed his grip I became terrified and scrambled down the ladder, away from him.

"I'll meet you two tomorrow, by the fence!" he called down after us in the friendliest of tones.

"We don't have to play with him anymore," Billy said, trying to reassure me as I ran wide-eyed through the brambles which got caught on my clothes and hair and scratched at my bare arms. He gingerly held back the prickly vines for me as he led the way back to our lawn.

"But it's too bad 'cause he sure has a nice tree house," he added with longing.

"WELLSOMEWHEREINTHEBLACKMOUNTAINSHILLSOF SOUTHDAKOTATHERELIVEDAYOUNGBOYNAMEDROCKY RACOOOO-OOOOON!" The three Smith girls were shouting at the top of their lungs at the children's dinner table in the pale kitchen that looked out onto the sunny green lawn.

"Ay, ay, ay," our nanny Candida said, covering her ears after she flipped the steaks in the frying pan.

"ANDONEDAYHISWOMANRANOFFWITHANOTHER GUYHITYOUNGROCKYINTHEEEEYE . . ."

"You sing terrible," Billy said, gazing uncomfortably at his soup.

"It's the *Beatles*, you fool." Cassandra lit a cigarette and pushed her bowl toward the middle of the table. As soon as the parents went out she started smoking in the house.

"I'm bored," she said. "I'm so boooooored."

"We can walk down to the boardwalk after dinner and see if those cute guys are there again tonight," Mary-Ellen said enigmatically. Mary-Ellen was a little fat, her hips were too wide, her face too flat and round. But her eyes were big and had long red lashes, and she had the prettiest hair of anybody, long and golden red. She had a tight little mouth which told you that she disapproved of everything but would never lower herself to speak out.

Mary-Ellen had ignored me since the first day, with a practiced vehemence I found hard to swallow. She snorted every time I spoke and looked at me through her long lashes as though I were a dead bird one of my mother's cats had dragged in. She hated me more than the other two put together. I could not figure out why.

"She's jealous of you," Billy would say as though it were the simplest thing in the world.

Jealous of me? I could not imagine why Mary-Ellen would be jealous of *me*. I could understand if she were jealous of her older sister, who was thin as a willow and very grown-up and always right about everything, and of her younger sister who was adored by everyone. The grown-ups thought Gillis was brilliant because she said such grown-up things. I thought the grown-ups were completely stupid because it only took me three days to realize that Gillis was only parroting her older sisters, that none of the brilliant expressions she spewed out were her own.

I decided after a few weeks that if Mary-Ellen was jealous of me it was because *I* was not the plain one between two gorgeous and supposedly brilliant sisters; I only had a normal brother who was as gentle and nice as could be. And maybe she was a little jealous because I was thin as well and could speak French. I could tell Mary-Ellen was dying to learn French because she practiced words when no one was listening.

"I WANNA COME TO THE BOARDWALK TOO," Gillis screamed at the dinner table. "I WANNA DRAAG!"

"Here." Cassandra handed her the cigarette. "Just one drag, now," she said. The little Princess Child with the long golden hair and cherubic face puffed on the cigarette, turning the coal bright red, and inhaled deeply. She blew smoke rings into the air.

"Ay, ay, ay," Candida said, muttering in French in her Portuguese accent, "that littla one es only ten jears old!"

"MY GOD, Cassandra, I swear this time I'm telling!" Bethany, their nanny, said in dismay. Bethany's hair was all frizzed out and she wore too much makeup.

"Then I'll tell Mom you smoked pot with Fred in the garage and I caught you," Cassandra said.

"You're horrible," Bethany said.

"Oh, come on. I won't tell," Cassandra said coyly. She pulled her chair closer to Bethany's and started to caress her arm, begging her to let them go down to the boardwalk. Even if Bethany said no the two oldest would go, because the parents never came home until after midnight. Bethany, it seemed, never contradicted the Smith girls because she was as terrified of Mr. Smith as Candida was of our father.

That night, in my darkened room, I watched a tree swaying in the silver moonlight outside the window and thought of the boy in the tree house. A strange shiver crossed my body. My brother had defended me and offered not to play with him anymore, but the thing I wanted most in the world at that moment was to return to the tree house and allow the strange boy to kiss me again. I hugged Christmas Bear to my chest. He was huge, beige, and soft. I'd had to throw a major tantrum and forsake all my other toys to be allowed to bring him in the car from Paris. Christmas Bear knew all my thoughts. He knew I was not thinking of him that night, but of another boy, and I whispered to him to forgive me as I pressed my ear against his furry chest.

The next day my brother had to go to the doctor to have a boil removed from under his arm. I asked if I could go along but my parents thought I might start to cry and frighten Billy. So I stayed home and watched the Smith girls play croquet on the lawn.

Thoughts of the boy kept sending chills down my spine. I wandered off toward the woods involuntarily. It was the same strange urge I'd had when at three I'd walked into the deep end of a pool and almost drowned.

The boy was there, waiting. He was leaning with his arms outstretched against the fence.

"*Où est ton frère?*"

"He had to go to the doctor's."

We stared at each other in silence for a while. Without talking we walked, each on our side of the fence, to the place where the hole was. My brother's red handkerchief was still there. The boy held the chicken wire up and I passed through to his side. He took my hand in his big rough one and pulled me through the thickets toward his tree house. I watched carefully, feeling like Gretel without Hansel, for a tell-tale tree, a certain flowering vine, so that, in an emergency, I could find my way back to the fence.

"Go ahead, climb up first," he said.

Today I was wearing a skirt.

I thought about this for a second, feeling quite coy. With only a moment's hesitation I shimmied up the ladder. I sensed his eyes looking up at me from below and strange, uncomfortable shivers clambered up my spine.

I threw myself into a corner and turned so that I would be facing him. Soon he was beside me, peering at me with wolfish eyes.

"You want to hold my slingshot?"

It seemed slightly hypocritical for me to do so, but I was not planning to aim the thing, much less shoot at any small animals, so with just the right touch of unwillingness, I said, "All right."

"You see, it works like this." He held it up and pulled back on the elastic. "My father taught me how to make them." There was something tough and hard-edged about the way he manipulated the slingshot and the slightly gruff sound of his voice which made me think that this was not the pretend Cowboys and Indians game I played with Billy, this was the real thing.

"I'll make you one," he said.

"I don't want one," I said quickly.

"Want to see my snails?"

"Your snails?"

"Yes. I collect them."

"You don't hurt them, do you?"

"Of course not," he said as though I were completely stupid.

I had never been afraid of snails, I liked them. He brought a box out of another dark corner and placed it between us. It had leaves in it and mosquito netting over the top. He reached inside and soon there were three gray snails with brown and beige shells gliding slowly up his arm leaving thin, wet tracks.

"You want to hold one?"

"Sure," I said.

"Then take off your shirt."

"Why?"

"They feel really good on your chest and neck," he said simply.

Why not allow a snail to crawl along my chest? I lifted my shirt up over my head. He put a snail on my shoulder near my neck and then kissed me on the corner of the mouth. His lips were sweet and wet, like cherries. He had a strange, longing look in his eyes which made my stomach churn uncomfortably.

There I was, bare to the waist, with no breasts for him to touch. I wondered with a certain amount of envy whether he might not like Cassandra or Mary-Ellen better than me, if he ever got a look at them up close. I decided we must never invite him over to play at our house.

"Take off your skirt," he said slowly. He was pinching the hem in his dirt-stained fingers while he kissed the palm of my hand.

I did not want to take off my skirt. On the beach, I wore no top—no girls my age did in France. But to show him my white cotton panties up close was another story. But I did not want to anger him, either. I agonized over the decision.

"Promise me you'll never kill any more animals with your slingshot."

"I promise," he said flatly.

I convinced myself momentarily that it would not be terribly naughty of me to take off my skirt for a few seconds—it would be my sacrifice for the forest animals—

and off came the skirt. There I sat in his dark tree house in my white panties which felt scratchy from the dirt on the floor. As soon as I had removed it I felt completely exposed and my heart ached with dread because now he could hold something over me. After that, the boy and the tree house sank in a brownish haze and remained that way forever in my memory.

"Take them off, too," he said, nodding toward the panties.

"*Non.*"

"Take them off, I said."

"*Non.* I'll tell."

"Ha ha ha!" He laughed sordidly, kissing me again. "You want to see what I look like naked?"

"I already saw my brother naked," I said, a nervous edge beginning to strain my voice.

"That's not the same. Look."

His thing was pale and curved upward like an index finger crooked in a beckoning gesture. He grabbed my wrist and brought my hand toward it. The back of my hand grazed its mushroomlike head as I tugged to free myself. I screamed and kicked at his shins, snatching my shirt and skirt with my free hand. He tried to seize my clothes but my grasp was firm and I threw myself out of the tree house rather than let him have them. I managed to grip a few rungs of the ladder on my way down, which broke my fall. The earth below the tree was soft but my knees and palms were nevertheless badly scraped and bruised. I tore through the brambles and thickets in my bare skin, still gripping my clothes, crying so hard I could barely see.

It took me a while to find the red handkerchief, but the boy did not follow. I dressed quickly on my side of the fence and ran all the way to Candida, who was sitting in the kitchen snapping green beans. Candida took one look at me and blanched. Her olive-colored skin took on a greenish hue, which terrified me more and made me howl. She could do nothing to quiet me.

"Didi, Didi, Didi!" I cried.

"*Bébé, mon bébé,* what es happened to jou? What

happened to jou?" She sat me on the table. Her sharp nose and small brown eyes were inches from my face.

"I fell out of a tree," I sobbed. Candida got the bandaids and mercurochrome out of the pantry closet.

"Ay, ay, ay, Channa, why ara jou climbing trees by jourself?" She washed my knees and arms with a clean, warm and soapy rag. "Jou es crazy."

Whenever I cried, Candida's eyes filled with tears as well. And when she cried because she missed her mother and the dusty farm in Portugal, I cried as though it were my mother and my farm. At that moment I couldn't take her tears and cried all the harder, and Candida cried harder too, and we hugged each other, rocking from side to side. I wept because I was not telling her the truth and never could. Candida was scared to death of men, she often told me that all men wanted only one thing from a nice girl, and if she gave it to them, that made her a bad girl and then they wouldn't like her anymore.

"*God.*" It was nasty Mary-Ellen standing in the doorway. "What do we have *here*? Can I join the party?"

Candida could not have understood what Mary-Ellen said, but the look of utter mockery on her face said it all.

"*Sors d'ici tout da suita!*" Candida yelled. "Get out ofa here des minute!" Candida did not take mockery from anyone but me. None of the Smith girls had ever heard Candida raise her voice. She had a real fishwife's voice when she wanted, and Mary-Ellen fled, horrified.

"My poor littel girl," she said to me. "Whatta dida we do to get sucha bad girls des summer?"

Everyone was excessively nice to me that evening. My father tucked me into bed with Christmas Bear and told me that nothing was broken and I would be all right. I could have told my father what happened because my father always talked about Sex as a natural and good thing. But my father was a maniac when it came to protecting Billy and me, and I knew that he would have gone straight to the boy's house and beaten him up and probably his father as well. Once when I was two, a five-year-old boy who was visiting with his parents kicked me in the face when the grown-ups left us alone in the playroom. My father found me lying on the floor, staring up unblinkingly while my assailant's foot continued to bash into my bloody head. My father kicked the boy into a wall right in front of his protesting parents.

My father, I knew, would blame Stephane and not me because Stephane was much older and stronger. For some strange reason I did not want Stephane to get into trouble because of me. I did not want the thing to become a big scandal that the Smith girls would be privy to, or for my father to make it so final that I could never, ever see him or his tree house again. So I cried instead as my father tucked me in, and kept my mouth shut.

"He's bad, Billy," I told my brother the next day. "He's really bad."

"He's not that bad," Billy said, looking away impatiently.

"I'm not playing in the woods anymore," I said with finality.

"I am," Billy said, heading off on the great green lawn with a new handkerchief in his back pocket.

"BILLY, DON'T!" I yelled after him. "PLEASE DON'T!" But he would not stop to listen to me.

I waited awhile, feeling both ashamed and betrayed. The Smith girls were haw haw hawing on the lawn, as usual. After a few minutes I followed Billy into the woods. I wandered around aimlessly, talking to the Elves, and suddenly found myself in front of the hole in the fence.

I followed the sound of their boyish voices, apprehension filling my heart. Before I could see the tree house I heard them laughing. They did not notice me and I watched from behind a thicket as Stephane flung stones at the squirrels in the next tree. Then he handed the slingshot to Billy and Billy paused for a moment, his face wrinkled into a thoughtful frown. I waited, hoping he would put the slingshot down. He raised it, pulled back the thongs, closed one eye, and fired.

"Billy," I shouted, scrambling out of the underbrush.

He dropped the slingshot on the floor of the tree house and lowered his eyes guiltily.

Stephane picked up the slingshot, put in a new stone and aimed it at me.

"Girls aren't allowed in here!" he said. "Go away."

I should have taken this as a lesson for my teenage years but of course did not. I thought Stephane was crazy, that boys never behaved this way. It was a sad lesson when years later I realized that he had not been the exception but a small taste of things to come.

"You promised me," I said to Stephane, hissing at him.

"Fuck off," he said. Billy sat motionless, looking down at his feet.

In English, I asked my brother to please come back with me. Stephane, understanding the gist of it, said that my brother was a coward and a fag if he listened to me.

My brother stayed where he was, gazing at his feet.

I turned away and went back to the fence, feeling a rage and a hatred against the world that I had not known possible. I could not even cry I was so enraged. I went to find solace with Candida in the kitchen, but Candida, having no idea, only made me feel worse with her gentle words of affection.

When Billy came in an hour or so later, I stared at him from the table where I sat while he poured himself a glass of milk from the fridge. He gingerly approached the table, trying to decide whether or not to sit down. He smiled at me in a shy, guilty blush and fiddled with the back of the chair.

"You are not my brother," I said in English so that Candida would not understand, slowly, with more conviction and more vehemence than I had ever said anything in my life. "You are not my brother, you're a Frog and you will never be my brother. You're adopted and you're not their son. From now on I'm going to pretend you don't exist."

Billy continued to stare at his feet, his face drained of color. We heard a gasp then, and both turned to find Mary-Ellen standing in the doorway. Billy's face went from white to red in a second; very slowly, back erect, he walked past Mary-Ellen and out the door.

"Whatta you say, Channa?" Candida said, her dark eyes shifting from Mary-Ellen to me and back again. "Whatta you say to him?"

"I'm going to tell on you," Mary-Ellen said slowly, in a voice very much like the one I had just used on my brother. "You're not supposed to say things like that, I know, 'cause my parents told me all about it."

"I don't care," I said, mustering up the last drop of courage I had left. "I hate you too. You're fat and mean."

I walked past her, feeling her eyes digging into my back, and went to look for Billy.

I went up to his room, which was next to mine, at the end of one of the halls on the second floor. The door was closed. I knocked lightly on the door, afraid to disturb the fathers.

"Billy," I whispered. "Billy! Can I come in?" There was no response. They had taken the keys away from our doors because they were afraid we'd lock ourselves in, so I turned the knob and walked into his darkened room. He'd closed the shutters and slats of sunlight lay on top of him on the bed. He was lying facedown in the pillow, sobbing without a sound. I could see his shoulders shaking.

I sat down at his side and put a flat hand on his shoulder. He did not shrug me off as he usually did when I touched him.

"Billy," I said. "Billy, I didn't mean it, I swear it. You *are* my brother. You're the only brother I have and I'm so glad you're here, Billy, because you're so good and nice and those girls are so terrible."

He continued to sob into the pillow without a sound.

"That boy did something very bad to me yesterday while you were at the doctor's," I said. "He made me take my clothes off and then he took out his thing that didn't look like yours at all. At all."

His shoulders stopped shaking beneath my hand. He said something into the pillow I could not understand.

"What?" I said, my heart pounding that he had deigned to say anything to me at all.

"What did it look like?" he said sniffling, turning his head to the side, away from me.

"Like a finger," I said.

"Like a finger?"

"Yes. I was so scared, Billy, I jumped out of the tree

43

house and ran all the way home. That's how come I was mad. I wanted you to stick up for me like you do with those stupid girls."

"It's not fair," he said and let out a long and terrible sigh. "It's not fair that you can say things like that."

"I know," I said, and began to cry.

"You're just scared you're going to get into trouble with Daddy," Billy said.

"I'll go tell him right now, before Mary-Ellen does. I'll go tell him what I said so he can punish me."

"No, don't," Billy said. "She won't probably say anything anyway. Just go away, all right? Just leave me alone."

I went to my room and curled up with Christmas Bear. Sobs ripped from my chest into his furry body and I thought I was going to choke on my heart.

Everything seemed almost normalized by dinnertime. I had knocked on Billy's door and asked him to come downstairs with me to eat. The five of us children and our two nannies were sitting at the round table in the kitchen eating in silence when our fathers came in looking like two horrific thunderclouds.

"Channe," my father said evenly, "I heard something really terrible today."

Billy looked up from his plate, stopped chewing although his mouth was still full, and stared at me with horror in his big blue eyes. Candida got up and went to the stove. She always backed off when my father made such an entrance.

I glanced at Mary-Ellen. She was very erect, very pleased with herself as she daintily sliced a piece of meat with a bent wrist.

"Did Channe say something terrible to you today, Billy?" my father asked. "I'm not asking you what she said. But did she say something she's not supposed to say?"

Billy looked at me with those eyes and my own filled with tears, out of terror for myself, shame toward him, and hatred for Mary-Ellen. Billy looked quickly at Mary-Ellen, quickly at me, and then at the fathers standing by the

44

doorway. He swallowed his unchewed food with a loud gulp and then said,

"No," as though he were thinking hard to remember. He'd made a completely flat, innocent face, a face he'd probably learned from watching Gillis charm the parents.

"Channe didn't say a terrible thing to me today. We didn't have a fight since we came here from Paris," he said.

My father's mouth twitched into a peculiar smile. He must have known that Billy was lying, but the fact that he was sticking up for me must have meant more to him than the fact that I'd broken the iron rule.

"All right," he said, beginning to turn away.

"But Mary-Ellen came to me and told me she overheard something—" Mr. Smith began in a peeved tone.

"Mary-Ellen must of not heard right," Billy said flatly.

Mary-Ellen's eyes flashed lightning bolts at us. She was shaking with humiliation and fury.

"Little brats," she hissed. "God, do I hate brats."

The Smith girls did not turn out badly at all but I still don't like them. Close to twenty years have passed since that summer, and Cassandra is one of the most successful women I know. She makes over $300,000 a year as a stockbroker on Wall Street. She is not married. Mary-Ellen is still fat, much fatter, in fact, and is in Vienna training to become an opera singer. People who have heard her sing say she has a strong voice but sings slightly off key. Gillis, the Princess Child, is still a princess child. She married a very rich and very old film producer and lives in Beverly Hills with his two daughters who are at least five years her senior. Fortunately, none of the Smith girls are readers of fiction, or it would never have occurred to me to write this story.

HUMAN
DEVELOPMENT

R iding home on the public bus on the first Friday of the first week of 7ème, fifth grade, I came to a stupefying realization: There wasn't a teacher in the school or a student in my class who liked me.

It was a long bus ride home; usually Candida came to get me in the car but today she had an appointment with people from the government about her working papers, and my mother had an important tea. I was relieved to be alone, and sat on the quiet, not-so-crowded bus, pondering my realization for a long time.

It had been apparent since the first day of school that my reputation among the teachers had preceded me. But I asked myself, was I really all that bad? All that much worse than anybody else?

I figured I'd made one huge mistake with a teacher, and that had been in last year's history class.

We were studying ancient Greece for half the year. I already knew more than anybody about ancient Greece because the previous summer my father had taken the family to a tiny, hot Greek island. Since there was nothing to do on the island at night, he had read us the entire *Iliad* and *Odyssey* during the two-and-a-half-month vacation.

It seemed incredible and wonderful to me that my brother and I could understand every word our father read

46

out of the huge, leather-bound book he'd brought from Paris. One night I peeked over his shoulder as he was reading and saw that the words he said weren't always the ones written down. I remembered seeing, for example, "Exclaimed Ulysses" when he read "Ulysses cried out."

I became so enthralled by the gods and heroes that I wrote my favorite ones letters. My father ceremoniously burned the notes on a small pyre on the beach, to ensure that the messages would reach their destination.

"Dere Athena," I wrote, "I am youre friend. I am so happie you like the Greeks and not the Trojans. Please send me a signe—Channe Willis."

Or, "Dere Achilles, My daddie says demi-gods are not imortelle but I am writing you any way. Will you merry me if I die and go to Hadies?—Channe Willis."

Last year's history teacher had been very young and nervous, and boring. She had red hair tied in a large knot at the back of her head and a face so pale she almost disappeared when she stood against the white wall. Her voice was flat and quiet, even when she described battles. Then one day she made a terrible mistake while drawing the battle of Troy on the blackboard with colored chalk. She said that Athena whisked Paris away and saved his life as Agamemnon was about to slaughter him in front of the gates of Troy.

"It wasn't Athena!" I yelled out, "it was Aphrodite!" The teacher turned as red as her chignon and mumbled, *"Et bien, Mademoiselle*, maybe you would like to instruct the class, since you obviously find me unfit for the task."

I felt terrible and wanted to apologize (even though I was right), but it was too late. After that I tried to be polite and apply myself, but between us it was war.

When I discussed this with my father, he explained that not all grown-ups behaved like grown-ups. The bigger you got, he said, the bigger your ego got.

"Try to be nice to her," he suggested, "let her feel she knows more than you."

But the teacher continued to give me five out of tens on all my tests and projects no matter how hard I tried.

* * *

So—this year they had been ready for me—they chided me for my big, bad mouth, my bossiness, my pushiness, and my flirtatious nature (no one knew the extent of my flirtatious nature, thank God). In the last two years I had convinced every cute boy in my grade to show me their thing behind a park bench during recreation.

My mind drifted to the question of their thing for a moment. The American boys' all looked like a little pale mushroom, while the French boys' looked like a garlic clove before you peeled it. For a while I'd believed that it had to do with where you were born (my brother was born in France and had a garlic clove, whereas my father was born in America and had a mushroom). But then I discovered one American boy born in America who had a garlic clove instead of a mushroom, and my theory was shattered. I still contemplated asking my father to explain, but hadn't quite figured out how to ask him so that it wouldn't sound like I'd seen more than two.

My thoughts went back to my teachers and to the nasty, underhanded comments they had been throwing in my direction since the first day of school: "Apparently your vacation hasn't calmed you down;" or, "Always as disruptive, I see." My new math teacher even said, "You aren't stupid—why do you insist on pretending you are?"

How did they know if I was stupid or not?

It wasn't fair. They never picked on the other dummies in the same way.

In math, certainly, I really was stupid. Even the most simple problems baffled me, and then last year they'd made things unbearable by introducing division. Feeling frustrated and victimized, I'd given up listening to the teacher and taken to tickling my best friend Sally Sutherland, who sat next to me. In my lassitude I also wrote love notes in French to Paul Frankel, a boy with fantastically dark eyes who happened to sit at the next desk. "Paul, if you kiss me after class, I will give you my Pez candies," I would write. He always wanted to know what Disney character I had as my Pez container and what flavor Pez I'd brought that day. He'd promise to kiss me in writing, I'd pass him my Pezes under the desk, and then afterward, in the hallway, sometimes he'd kiss me and sometimes he'd yank up my skirt.

I thought about Sally, how good she was. She never wrote notes to boys, always did her homework, and no one ever yanked up her skirt. My heart constricted painfully. It was a feeling of longing mingled with acute jealousy. This year I was in the dummy class, 7ème C, while Sally had stayed in 7ème A. Finally free of me, she was making a whole new batch of friends. I had never realized how much I depended on her, my quiet, funny, good-natured, sensible friend—or that she was my *only* friend—because it hadn't mattered up until now. The whole thing made me want to cry.

Sitting alone on the bus, I realized that although I hated the school and it hated me, I was used to it and was too much of a coward to change. I'd heard that in a French lycée, the teachers had a right to beat you, and you couldn't go to the bathroom during class. And there wouldn't be any Americans. But then, in a strictly American school like the one my brother went to, there would be no French kids, and I would seem so French that the other kids would hate me anyway.

No, the École Internationale Bilingue was the only school for me because almost all the kids were some kind of half-and-half. In that sense, I was no weirder than others.

By the end of that first week in 7ème C, I'd found that everyone had settled into distinct groups, and I was clearly being excluded, along with Frédérique Charpentier and Francis Fortescue, who were the weirdest kids I'd ever seen in my life.

Frédérique's parents were dead and she was being raised by her grandmother. Either because her grandmother didn't know any better or because Frédérique was emulating her, she dressed and acted like an old lady. She wore galoshes and knitted shawls, and her long blond braids were tied up around her head, which was shaped like a heart. She made silly granny-chuckles and wiped at her eyes with a lace hankie, walked slump shouldered, and—of all things!—she knitted during recreation in the park.

Francis Fortescue was a new student. Within a day he had usurped Frédérique's position, which she'd held for several years, as School Weirdo Number One, because he looked and behaved exactly like a girl. He had a fine, pretty face, black hair, and big eyes whose lashes were so long and dark they looked fake. His dainty white hands fluttered so that you wanted to tie them down behind his back.

By the end of the week, Frédérique and Francis had become fast friends. They had begun to pair up for the walk to recreation in the park. Watching them—her, slump shouldered and arthritic-looking, him traipsing daintily along—was so amusing that the rest of the class began to call them *"la mémère et sa petite-fille,"* the granny and her granddaughter.

Admittedly, I was no angel; I picked on them verbally as much as anybody, but had not—until that afternoon—raised a hand against them. It had not been a moral issue, only that physical violence nauseated me. But today during recreation, because I'd been in a particularly sour and envious mood, I'd pulled Frédérique's hair.

Frédérique had just been kicked in the shin by Luc Wang, a huge, half-Chinese boy with a square head; she was hopping around on one leg, crying with a comical, twisted-up face. She looked so ridiculous that I, feeling an odd rush of blood in my lower stomach that seemed to flood outward to my toes and fingertips, came up from behind and swiftly tore one of the braids loose. It fell in a stiff, curving shape onto her shoulder. The look of shock and despair that came over her face made me feel so horrible that my stomach began to come up. I had to go sit on the ground with my back against a tree.

A fight then broke out between Francis Fortescue and Luc. Old Francis spun around and cried out in a high-pitched voice, "I'm tired of you, you big bully!" and slapped Luc hard across the face with a flat hand. While he stood leaning on one hip with his arms crossed, Luc, stunned, came at him with fists, and Francis went absolutely crazy. He started screaming like a wild monkey, doing a dance that looked very much like the Charleston I had seen in *Thoroughly Modern Millie*. He slapped, kicked, and scratched his opponent in a mad flailing of arms and legs. Luc, bewildered, embarrassed, his face like a big strawberry, fled.

Once Francis had calmed down he approached me (I was still recuperating by my tree) and said in perfect American, "And *you*," pointing, "*you* should be ashamed of yourself. What did that poor girl ever do to *you*?"

I was so upset I couldn't speak. While Francis marched off to console Frédérique, it crossed my mind that I hadn't even known Francis was American; his last name was so weird and his French was so good.

Just as I was considering apologizing (in secret) to Frédérique and Francis, someone approached from the back of the bus and took the seat beside me. Out of the corner of my eye I saw Francis. He was sitting primly, arms resting on his *cartable*, legs crossed, staring straight ahead as though his presence were entirely accidental and he hadn't seen me.

"I didn't know you were American," I said in a neutral voice, as an opening.

"You don't know *any*thing about me but I know a lot about *you*," he said in an annoying, mysterious way.

I turned toward the window. This was the longest bus ride in the world. My parents didn't like for me to take public transportation by myself, but it would do in an emergency. I liked the bus much better than the metro although it took much longer, because it was less crowded and went practically straight to my door.

"Yes," Francis continued in his loud, high-pitched voice, "For example I know you live on Île Saint-Louis. I know you go to boulangerie on Rue des Deux Ponts on your way home and sometimes on Saturdays."

"How do you know that?" I said, frowning at him. He had a nasty little gleam in his eyes.

"Because I *live* on Rue des Deux Ponts," he said. "You *never* look around you when you walk. You walk with your nose down like a nun."

We rode on for a while in silence.

"My mother says I should talk to you about sharing a ride with you. My mother would take us in the morning and then someone from your house could pick us up at night. Or the other way around. Whatever floats your boat."

"Maybe," I said vaguely.

"You know, you're not particularly nasty, really. Why did you do that today to Frédérique? You just up and flipped your lid, or what?"

"I don't know." The way he talked made me want to laugh for some reason: whatever floats your boat, walk with your nose down like a nun, up and flipped your lid. I hadn't felt so curious in a long time, and curiosity always had a way of lifting my spirits.

"Poor Frédérique," Francis said thoughtfully, and sighed. "She's such a dope, really."

"Why are you friends with her if you don't like her?"

"Oh she's okay. You know how it is. Walking *with* somebody to recreation is always better than walking alone." This seemed profound to me, it touched on something that was disturbing me too.

"I have a dog and a tropical aquarium," Francis said. "What do you have?"

"My mother has three Siamese cats."

"My mother has a Deux-Cheveaux. What do your parents have?"

"A Peugeot 404."

"I'm crazy about opera and I'm learning the violin."

Opera? I thought. I knew that it had to do with singing but hadn't the vaguest notion of it otherwise.

"What kind of name is that, Fortescue?"

"American. It's my mother's maiden name. I don't know my father's. It could have been Rumpelstiltskin for all I know." He shrugged exaggeratedly and turned his eyes upward, under his fluttering lids.

I laughed. "You're weird. You act like a girl."

"I don't act *like* anybody," he said, "I act like me. And I know everything about sex and things already. My mother told me."

"If you know everything then tell me this," I said, and lowered my voice, even though we were speaking English.

52

"Tell me why the zizis of American boys are round while the zizis of French boys are pointed."

"It's got nothing to do with if you're French or American," Francis explained matter-of-factly. "It has to do with which hospital you're born in and also if you're Jewish or Catholic or Protestant. My mom says it's called circumcision. She says if you're Catholic, they cut a tiny piece of skin off the end, see, and if you're Jewish or Protestant, they don't. No, wait—maybe it's the other way around—if you're Jewish, they cut a tiny piece of skin off . . ."

"I don't believe you," I said, squinting at him. It was more for effect than because I didn't believe him.

He shrugged. "What do I care if you believe me or not, it's the truth."

I thought of all those zizis I'd seen and wondered how it could be that none of those boys were my friends at all, not even enough so that I could ask them such a simple question.

After a short silence, Francis told me he'd like to invite me over to see his aquarium and his dog but that he had to ask his mother first. I told him proudly that I didn't have to ask anybody and invited him to come over and have a *pain au chocolat* for *gouter*.

Over the weekend, Francis met my parents and my brother Billy, and I met Francis's mother, his dog, and his tropical fish. He had named every single fish in the tank and could tell them apart. The tank was the only clean thing in the entire apartment. The dog was the ugliest and stupidest dog I'd ever seen, a medium-sized white one with brown and black spots and no tail. You could call it for half an hour and it still wouldn't come to you.

Mrs. Fortescue had long, knotty dark hair streaked with gray, the same black eyes with long lashes as her son, and a big stomach that made her look pregnant. Her sweater had holes in it and so did her pants and sneakers.

It looked like a storm had come through their apartment, which had a white linoleum floor and no rugs and dog hair everywhere. It looked like dog and it smelled like dog. Opera blasted through the main room, making the windows rattle. This was Mrs. Fortescue's bedroom and the living room. The connecting room was empty except for boxes and a large, square table. On the table lay an enormous, flat piece of wood. Apparently they were building a train set, complete with mountain ranges, cow pastures, and Swiss villages. The work was going slowly. Francis said they'd started last spring. I contemplated the surrounding mess and was impressed, because in my house such disorder would never have been permitted.

Francis's room was off down the hall. He owned three string puppets, two women and a man. One of the ladies was blond, wore a pink gown with gold trim and the other was in dark purple with silver trim and had black hair. Francis told me Esperanza was the good one, the one in pink, and Serpentina was the "evil adulteress, murderess, and home-wrecker." The little man was Don Francesco. "He's kind, fragile, and believes anything they tell him," Francis explained. "He always gets stuck in the middle between them and someone gets killed."

They looked so alive sitting on Francis's desk, staring with their lidded eyes, that they frightened me. I would not have liked to sleep with them staring at me like that.

Back at my place, at Saturday lunch, Candida hovered behind us like a big worried bird; her arms swooped down on the table and our shoulders from time to time, like giant wings. "Hi hi hi!" Francis giggled, hands fluttering. He flirtatiously slapped my brother's shoulder once in a while and said, "My, my, are you a shy one!" and Billy would make an unhappy face. It seemed to me that Francis was just playing the game that was expected of him, but it didn't seem obvious to Billy at all.

Sunday evening, my parents discussed the ride situation over the telephone with Mrs. Fortescue, and by Monday, Francis and I were inseparable.

We arrived at school in Mrs. Fortescue's Deux-Cheveaux. It was the messiest and noisiest tin can of a car I had ever been in in my life. There was so much dog hair on the seats that you could barely see the plaid pattern on the seatcovers; in the way back were empty yogurt containers that smelled like rotten milk, and paper wrappers from Eskimo popsicles with dog hair stuck to the melted chocolate. When I got out, the back of my blue blazer was covered with dog hair. I kept thinking on my way into the school that my father would have a heart attack if he ever saw Mrs. Fortescue's car or apartment. I thought it would be a good idea to avoid such a situation for as long as possible.

Francis ceased completely to show interest in Frédérique. He wasn't cruel but simply no longer acknowledged her existence. I felt sorry for her and saved a space for her at the next desk so that she wouldn't have to sit alone. But the more friendly I was, the more nasty and obnoxious she became. It was the oddest behavior I had ever encountered. Frédérique had something condescending and unpleasant to say about everything, as though she really believed she possessed a grandmotherly wisdom that gave her the right to attack everyone else's way of life. "You're so childish," she would say, clap her hands and cackle derisively. Or, if I would offer her a sweet, she'd shake her head, lowering her eyes, and say, "You should really be ashamed, eating things like that."

"You're a real drag, Frédé, you know that?" I said after a few days, not in a nasty way, but just as a statement of fact. She stared at me flatly with her pale eyes and said nothing. A few weeks later she came down with pneumonia and left the school forever.

About a month into the trimester, the headmistress came to our class with a questionnaire for the English-speaking students. A rumor had been going around the school (spread by the upperclassmen) that certain English-speaking parents were complaining to the administration. English was being taught as a foreign language even to American and English students, meaning that the school only had to hire one teacher—who was not even a native English speaker. It was not a daily class, but met twice a week, and all students were thrown in together. The school was saving money in this department, it was true, and everyone knew it. The English classes were so boring and easy that Francis and I were constantly getting thrown out into the hall, which was fine with us, since it gave us more privacy to talk and giggle. Francis had begun to tell me opera stories.

"Which opera would you like to hear today?" Francis would say while we stood out in the hall among the hanging coats.

"Tell me *Tosca* again."

He would proceed to tell me every detail of the love triangle and act out the characters' tragic and violent deaths. Francis never played the records for me or told me about the composers, just the stories. *Don Giovanni, Tosca, Aïda, Madame Butterfly, Otello, La Bohème;* they were the most wonderful, romantic, passionate, tragic stories I'd ever heard. I especially liked *Romeo and Juliet* and *Tosca.* When Francis would get to the end of *Romeo and Juliet* he'd say, "And then she *plunged* the dagger into her own breast," and pantomime plunging the dagger into his breast. Then he'd collapse into a heap of bones on the floor. For the end of *Tosca,* he'd jump off a table or throw himself downstairs if any were nearby.

The day the questionnaire was handed out by Madame Beauvier, *directrice,* Francis and I were sitting, as usual, in the very last row of desks.

"I see you two are still occupying the North Pole," the *directrice* said in a pointed tone.

The questionnaire asked the students to write down their parents' names, nationalities, how many years they'd been in France, and so on. Feeling important, I busily wrote in that my parents were American but that I was born in France and had always lived in France. Since there were only four English-speaking students in 7ème C, Madame Beauvier gathered the questionnaires quickly and took a moment to glance over them as she stood near the door.

"Francis Fortescue," she said in her loud, determined voice. "You have forgotten to put down your father's name and nationality."

Francis looked up at the ceiling, eyelids fluttering, and tapped his fingers impatiently on the desk top.

"What is your father's name, Francis?" The *directrice*'s

mouth became a hard little knot as she positioned her clipboard in the crook of her arm and raised a pencil to Francis's questionnaire.

Can't she see she's embarrassing him? I thought. Can't she just go away?

"Well, we're waiting, Francis," Madame said. "We don't have all day."

Everyone turned to stare at Francis.

"I don't know," Francis finally said in an exasperated tone, and glared back at the *directrice*.

"You don't know?" she repeated, and shook her head slightly. "Well, that explains everything, doesn't it?" she concluded with confidence, as though she'd suspected as much all along.

Everyone tittered, including the teacher, who already did not think highly of Francis or me. Then Madame Beauvier left, telling the class sharply as she stood in the doorway that we were all a bunch of bandits and better learn to behave or else.

I glared at the words I'd written on my notebook just before Madame Beauvier came in. It was a dictation, some complicated passage from *Les Misérables*. I was so distraught I couldn't read the words or look at Francis for a long time. After a while he mumbled, "That bitch was just trying to get my goat."

One weekend we built an opera house for Francis's puppets, out of a large rectangular cardboard box. We constructed the sets out of all kinds of materials—Francis's mother's old scarves, dishrags, and veils; we bought velvet, marble, gold, and silver paper by the centimeter at the art supply store to decorate the walls and floor. Once we'd created a set, we'd lead the puppets through the complicated love triangles we'd invented for them. The sets changed more often and more radically than the stories.

Twice a week, Francis had his violin lesson, and only on those afternoons would we not get together after school. Those were lonely and boring afternoons for me.

"Practicing is so boring," Francis would say in a whiny

voice on those days, "but my mother says if I keep practicing I'll become a great violinist."

"For my birthday, my mother wants to take us to *Tristan and Isolde* at the opera," he announced to me one day on the way to recreation. "It's by Wagner, it's five hours long and there's barely any scenery. Do you think you can sit still that long? My mother thinks you're impatient and that it might be hard for you."

This statement made me decide immediately that I wouldn't move an inch through the whole opera if it killed me.

When I told my parents what we were doing for Francis's birthday, they looked at me in silence, without commenting. It seemed a bit odd to them, certainly, but how could they complain? At least it was a major step up from playing Cowboys and Indians in the street.

We sat in a loge on the right side of the opera house. There was no scenery but the inside of a ship's bow at the back of the slanting stage, and a few benches and some large trunks of Isolde's scattered here and there, on which the singers sat from time to time. I knew the story: In Act I Tristan is taking Isolde by ship to meet her future husband the King.

Tristan and Isolde were so very large that it seemed a bit strange to me—I imagined all tragic heroes should be young and skinny. It took Tristan and Isolde an hour and a half to accidentally drink the love vial destined for Isolde and her future husband the King, and then, at the close of the act, they threw themselves into each other's arms and the scenery trembled from the impact.

I sat still through the entire opera. On the way out, Mrs. Fortescue smiled down at me in her impish way and asked, "How did you like it?"

"I loved it," I said simply. "But they were a bit fat."

One day, Francis's mother brought his violin to school, and the teacher made time for him to play for a few minutes at the end of class.

"Now, children, Francis has brought his violin and is

going to play for us," the teacher said in a tone that sounded slightly derisive. Mrs. Fortescue stood by the door with her arms crossed, smiling at everyone as though she thought we were all so sweet and cute.

No one had ever done such a brash thing in the dummy class. Francis slowly, unhappily dragged himself to the front of the room and stood with his back to the blackboard, tapping his foot impatiently and making that condescending face, his eyes focused on the ceiling and his mouth puckered up as though his tongue tasted terrible to him.

He played a little classical piece slowly, without rhythm or nuance. Afterwards, everyone clapped politely and his mother left with his violin.

"That was good, Francis," I said.

"No it wasn't. You don't have an ear for music, you can't tell. It was lousy. I don't play well. My mother likes me to play, though. It was her idea, not mine. Maybe I should take voice lessons, or try the piano instead? I'm going to have to learn to do *some*thing musical if I want to make it in the opera business."

I decided that I would ask my parents if Francis could spend the night during Christmas vacation. I waited until we were all gathered for dinner one evening.

"Can Francis sleep over next weekend?"

My parents looked at each other quickly and then at me.

"Where's he going to sleep?" my mother asked.

"He can sleep in Billy's room," I suggested.

"What are you, nuts?" Billy said, glaring at me. Our father laughed out loud, throwing his weight back in the chair, which tipped.

"Watch the Louis Treize furniture," our mother said. "That fat drunken jerk friend of yours ruined one already last month."

"He can sleep on the cot in your room," my father said, righting himself, still laughing.

It was a cot we sat on to watch TV. It stretched out to a single bed when you added the back-pillows to the end of the mattress. No one had ever slept on it before, but it was a good suggestion.

"We'll put the cot at the foot of my bed so he won't feel so far away," I said.

Francis began to sleep over often. We stayed up until dawn, making secret expeditions to the kitchen, giggling and telling ghost stories which naturally ended very badly for all the heroes involved.

On the first Monday of the second trimester, a new English class for fluent students was instituted in 7ème. It met five times a week. The new teacher was a young, black-haired Irish woman with eyes the color of stormclouds. She had a lovely face with pale skin that wrinkled easily when she smiled.

She told us that her name was Sheila O'Shaunessy, which was unusual in that teachers never volunteered their first names. In fact, it was a big deal if you could discover a teacher's first name. But there was Sheila O'Shaunessy, who spoke in an English I had never heard before. It didn't seem she was speaking so much as singing, her voice was so beautiful.

She read us lengthy ballads and Irish fairy tales about wily drunks, terrible dragons, damsels in distress, leprechauns, and pots of gold buried beyond the rainbow.

"I am from Belfast," she told us one day, in a heavy voice. This meant nothing to us. Sometimes when she told us about Ireland her eyes would brim with tears but she would quickly wipe them away. Then she would smile and say, "We have our troubles but we do love a happy Irish story," and open one of her many volumes of fables and fairy tales.

One day she talked about the torture of political prisoners and told us that the last thing people did before they died under torture was urinate. This fact bothered me so much that I went home and asked my father about it. He was perplexed, and fascinated that a teacher would talk so openly about such things.

"I'd like to meet your Miss O'Shaunessy," my father said.

One of the reasons I liked Miss O'Shaunessy's class was that I was reunited with my beloved friend Sally Sutherland.

Sally was as intelligent and studious as ever, and being quite levelheaded, did not resent my friendship with Francis at all.

But Francis became furiously jealous of Sally and of Miss O'Shaunessy and turned out to be the laziest and most disruptive student in the class.

Miss O'Shaunessy didn't seem to know anything about my reputation, and I believed that even if she had, she was the kind of person who would have given anybody a fair chance. I wanted to do well in Miss O'Shaunessy's class, and listened attentively and raised my hand whenever a question was posed that I could answer. And since I was listening for once, I could answer a good many questions. Whenever Miss O'Shaunessy smiled at me, my heart skipped a beat.

Miss O'Shaunessy did not give us dictations or stupid sentences to write over and over again, she allowed us to create our own stories. "Write about a summer vacation," she would say. Or, "Make up a story of your own."

My first essay was about a little girl who wakes up in the middle of the night to find that all her dolls and bears have come alive and are running away. They're angry at the way she treats them, because she piles them up in a corner of the room under the stairway and forgets their names. When she wakes up they have taken her top sheet, torn it into strips and made knots at each end, and are climbing out the window, down the three stories to the street. She runs to the window and leans out, crying and begging them to forgive her. After a short discussion they come back. The next morning she wakes up and finds her top sheet gone and all the dolls and bears in bed with her.

Miss O'Shaunessy gave me an A and wrote: "You have a most wonderful imagination! Now you must concentrate on your spelling. *Come* in English, not *comme*. A teddy *bear*, not a teddy *bare*. Learn your words and try not to think in French. This is a good way to remember *here* and *hear*: Here is a place, like w*here?—there;* to hear is in your *ear*."

Sally got a B+, although there were very few red marks on her essay, and Francis got a C. Sally's essay was about her gerbils. Francis wrote about how much he hated École Internationale Bilingue.

"You're just a damn teacher's pet," he said to me, making his disgusted face.

For some reason, this made me feel proud and wonderful. I redoubled my efforts toward participation and spelling. My first weekly report card brought me an A for *travail*, A+ for *éffort*, and an A for *comportement*.

After that, Francis started fighting with me in class. I wasn't *so* used to being good that I could avoid responding to the badgering. Miss O'Shaunessy didn't say anything for the first few days, but looked at us with her sad, gray eyes. Her eyes weren't anything like my nanny Candida's, which were round and chocolate-brown, but the expression of hurt and betrayal was so similar that they made me want to cry with vexation.

Finally Miss O'Shaunessy threw us out into the hall.

Francis tried to appease me by telling me another opera story.

"I've got a real good one for you today," Francis said, approaching me from behind while I hid my face in the hanging blue coats. "It's called *La Traviata* and I've been saving it for a special occasion."

But I was so angry I covered my ears and refused to talk to him.

Next week's essay was "Write about a friend of yours." I wrote:

Dear Miss O'Shaunessy,
My frende Francis is verry strange. He has no father and is verry nerveous. But some times he is verry smart and funny. But he allways wants to have attention and dosent know wen to stopp acting stupide. Your the best teachor I ever hade at this school and I am sory that I got kicked out of your class. Will you come to tea at my hous one day because my father and mother want to meat you because they cant' beleeve I got an A in your class.
    Youre frende and studente Channe Willis

Miss O'Shaunessy called me in for a private conference to discuss matters. Miss O'Shaunessy said she understood my friendship with Francis perfectly well, but she said in her beautiful singing, gentle voice,

"If Francis is truly your friend he will understand that he must not disrupt your studies."

And this is precisely what I said to Francis that afternoon, as Candida drove us home. Candida didn't understand English well enough to keep up with us when we spoke rapidly, and after I made my statement, Francis sat pouting against the door, as far away from me as he could get.

"Stop acting stupid, Francis," I said. "If I want to study in her class, I have a right to. You're just messing it up for me on purpose."

"That's a lot of crapola," he said. "And what about *you*? *You* never want me to go to violin class and *you* disrupt my practicing *every day*."

"You don't *like* to practice the violin, Francis. It's different. Anyway, you can practice at night after dinner."

"After dinner I'm too tired to practice, after running around in the street and playing opera with *you*, my head's too full of whirlygigs."

I considered the alternatives. I thought about my terrible, bossy nature, my big mouth, my lack of friends, and Miss O'Shaunessy. I wanted to change my bad ways—yet I did not want to go back to being alone the way it was before Francis. *But*—philosophically speaking, things could never quite go back to the way they were because now there was Miss O'Shaunessy and if I continued to apply myself, with Miss O'Shaunessy's help, I might even get moved back out of the dummy class. My friendship with Francis was solid and meant a lot to both of us, I knew. I did not believe he would be willing to give it all up—our opera stories, Saturday nights, our morning and afternoon rides, among other things, over Miss O'Shaunessy's class—so I gambled on this:

"If you don't leave me alone in Miss O'Shaunessy's class, then you're not really my friend. Because if you're really my friend, you'd help me. So I won't be your friend anymore unless you quit bugging me in Miss O'Shaunessy's class."

When Candida stopped in front of his apartment building, Francis got out and slammed the door. We watched his back as he slinked off, his head sagging unhappily, dragging his *cartable* by its strap.

"Whatta jou say to him?" Candida asked, frowning as she turned her head toward me in the backseat.

"Nothing bad. You know my new English teacher I told you about? I told him to stop bothering me in her class, that's all."

"Good girl," Candida said, nodding with approval. "That one es a wild dog. You es a wild dog too. Two wild dogs es enough to make any saint crazy. What happened to you friend that nice quiet fat littel girl? Why not play with her again instead? You know I esleep badly and I'm sick and tired of you two wild dogs howling at the moon all night every Saturday night."

Candida liked everything in life to be clear as day, pure as rain. Anything out of the ordinary threw her into a suspicious, gloomy temper. She had not liked Francis from the start and had just been waiting for the proper opportunity to express her feelings.

"Shut up, Didi," I said lightly. "You don't know what you're talking about."

Candida shook her head and drove away, hitting the gas with her lead foot and forgetting, as usual, to look in the rearview mirror.

The next morning Mrs. Fortescue picked me up, and I began to dread this ride before I even got in the car because Francis was sitting in front, staring out of the window with a sour look on his face. It would have been better if it were one of Candida's mornings, but as fate would have it, it was a Mrs. Fortescue morning and I got in the back and didn't say a word. No one said anything and so started the day.

After lunch (Miss O'Shaunessy's class was after recreation) Francis gingerly approached me as we were all pairing up for the walk to the park, and said,

"All right. I won't sit with you anymore in Miss O'Shaunessy's class. All *right*?"

"All right," I said. And we paired up as usual, feeling relieved.

The strain this ultimatum put on our relationship was not apparent to me for a long time. Just before the summer, the administration offered to move me back to the A group, and I accepted enthusiastically. Miss O'Shaunessy's attitude toward teaching had so influenced me that it had begun to affect my work in other classes. Only when I absolutely abhorred the teachers—the ones, of course, who were more predisposed than others to disliking me—did I refuse to apply myself in any way.

The following year, the native speakers of English were permitted to take history and geography in English as well. This second new teacher was almost as fabulous as Miss O'Shaunessy. She was a Canadian called Mrs. Dubois. She pronounced her name Duboy, and took great pleasure in correcting the French administrators. Her straight, brown hair was parted in the middle and constantly falling over her glasses. She wore large, flowing hippie dresses with cowboy boots. Her voice was incredibly loud; she always seemed to be yelling although she was never angry, only very demanding. "ALL RIGHT ALL YOU ENGLISH-SPEAKING FOLKS, WE'RE GONNA STUDY AMERICA THIS YEAR. GET READY TO WORK 'CAUSE BY THE END I'LL WANT YOU TO KNOW THE NAMES OF EVERY BLASTED RIVER AND LAKE AND STATE AND CAPITAL IN THAT CONTINENT, NORTH, CENTRAL, AND SOUTH."

The nature of my relationship with Francis did not change on the outside—although now we were in different classes. We played hopscotch together during recreation, sat together on the bus during outings, shirked during gym, and continued to invent opera stories and to go to the opera on special occasions.

But emotionally, it seemed that the scales had tipped. What had begun in Miss O'Shaunessy's class had become a pattern: I could set any ground rules I pleased in the relationship, and after a bitter argument, Francis would capitulate. Francis had come to depend on me more than I did on him, as had once been the case between Sally and me. And Francis had begun to resent me in the same way that I had resented Sally.

My flirtatious nature began to come out of its dormant stage with the budding of my breasts (which everyone, including my father, told me were large for my age). I wanted a bra because all the American girls wore them, even when they didn't need one. My mother and father gave this some thought and then suggested I wait awhile. My father said my breasts would probably get very big, like my mother's, and that the reason my mother's were in such good shape was because she'd refused to wear a bra as a young girl.

"And that's the truth, so help me God," my mother said, nodding and crossing her heart. "And *I* had the nuns to contend with."

Not wearing a bra allowed the muscles to develop, my father said.

"But do what you want," my mother added. "If you want boobies down to your knees, that's your affair."

If they had said, no, absolutely no bra, I would have most probably run to the first lingerie store. But pondering the matter, I decided that I did not want breasts that fell to my knees, so I listened to them.

Boys whom I'd known since kindergarten (many whose zizis I'd seen a while back) began to show a renewed interest in me. During recreation they chased me around the park, to Francis's great discomfort. It was easy, however, to flirt in certain classes because Francis was only in class with me for English with Miss O'Shaunessy, music with Mr. Flowers, and history/geography with Mrs. Dubois.

Suddenly, my classmates began inviting me to the *boums*, the Saturday evening parties where the lights were turned down low and the kids danced and kissed to the latest 45s from England. Francis was not invited and I did not discuss the matter with him. I did not know if he was aware of the *boums*' existence, and I did not want to find out.

At one *boum*, a boy accidentally touched my breast while we were slow dancing, and I said nothing. At the next *boum*, two different boys did the same thing and I reconsidered getting a bra.

"Francis," I asked him the next day as we were roller skating on the newly built bridge that was closed to traffic and connected the Île Saint-Louis to the Île-de-la-Cité, "Do you think my boobs are really all that much bigger than most of the other girls'?"

"How the hell should I know?" said Francis, shrugging.

"Do you think I should wear a bra? The other girls, the American ones, they tell me in the locker room that I definitely need a bra."

"My mother says American girls would wear chastity belts if someone told them it was the proper thing to do," Francis said. "Do what you want. But definitely I would tell those girls to mind their own beeswax."

I got my period for the first time on October 30, 1972, in music class. I had been feeling a dull ache in my lower stomach and back for several hours, and then, in the middle of singing "Let It Be," accompanied by Mr. Flowers on his portable electric piano, a warm wetness flooded my underwear. It was apparent to the more sophisticated students, who were all preoccupied with sex, that Mr. Flowers was as gay as Mardi Gras. He wore shirts with puffy sleeves and curled his hair and talked with a lisp. So I sat paralyzed in my seat, wishing this were Miss O'Shaunessy's class, or Mrs. Dubois's. To make things worse, Sally Sutherland was out sick with the flu. I was sitting next to Francis, which was fine in music class because he loved music class and got along famously with Mr. Flowers. After a moment I moved to the side in my chair and saw the beginnings of a brownish-red puddle on the shiny wooden seat, let out a tiny cry and whispered to Francis:

"Shit, Francis, I just got my period. What am I supposed to do!"

We'd talked about this eventuality quite often. Francis always had interesting insights on the question, which he'd gotten from his mother. For example, his mother told him I probably didn't have to worry for a few more years. However, my mother had been eleven when she got hers, and believed these things ran in the family.

"What should I do? What am I going to do!"

"You get up and go to the infirmary," Francis whispered. "And you say, 'I am indisposed.' That's what my mother told me you're supposed to do, anyway. I'll go with you and wait outside." Mr. Flowers came to the conclusion of "Let It Be" and Francis daintily raised his hand.

"Mr. Flowers," he said in a dead serious tone, "we must be excused."

Francis made the whole thing seem so normal that I'll remain grateful to him for this for the rest of my life. On the way to the infirmary he told me he'd taken his dog to "be fixed" because she too had gotten her period and that all these things were just regular occurrences and that I shouldn't be embarrassed.

That night at home, my father gave me one hundred francs in celebration, and a lecture on birth control. I stared at him in silence and nodded when I sensed he expected me to. I could not figure out at all what he was trying to get at. My mother also sat there, silently watching and listening.

My father then said the absolutely strangest thing I'd ever heard out of him:

"In my hometown we were already having sex with girls when we were ten. They were girls from the poor side of town. So I'm just saying, I'm not going to turn my back on this fact; boys are going to be interested in you and they're perfectly capable of going all the way already."

When I did not react, my mother said, "Your father isn't urging you to have sex, he's just warning you that you can get pregnant now."

Francis's voice started to change a few months later, and the tiny white hairs on his chin and under his nose began to turn black. This was not happening at all to my brother yet, and I did not know how to react. It had seemed so easy for Francis to deal with my period—why couldn't I deal with his? Saturday sleepovers became strange and awkward for me, and I had a difficult time falling asleep when Francis lay on the cot at the foot of my bed. After a while I stopped inviting him, and he did not mention the change.

A tow-haired boy fresh from America called Kevin Westgate arrived at the school halfway through the year. He did not speak a word of French and was put in a special class called Adaptation, which was supposed to be equal academically to the other classes but had a bad reputation and for some reason was kept segregated. Probably the French administration worried about the new American students' influence on the overprotected Europeanized students. At the time, people said that things in America were absolutely out of control; they said drugs were rampant as well as free sex and revolutionary attitudes.

Sally and I did not know how old this Kevin was but figured he was probably our age, or maybe just a little older, because he was in the Adaptation group that corresponded to 5ème, our grade, which would have been seventh back in America.

Sally and I would follow Kevin Westgate around the halls and then, when he'd turn around and gaze at us with a blank expression, we'd freeze. Once he'd disappear into the crowd of heads, we'd scream in unison like girls at a rock 'n' roll concert, and run in the opposite direction. We heard from other Adaptation students that Kevin was as shy and stupid as he was good-looking and hip. We were even told that he smoked pot.

One Sunday afternoon shortly after Kevin's arrival, Mrs. Fortescue took Francis and me to the opera to see *Madame Butterfly*. As the three of us were sitting all dressed up on the empty subway car, the most horrible coincidence in the world occurred. Kevin Westgate, accompanied by an older girl and younger boy who had the same tow-hair and little upturned nose and green eyes as he, got on the train and sat down across from us. Kevin's face lit up and he smiled, raising his hand in a wave. I automatically, without thinking, turned my face away and stared out the window. There, my own horrified face glared back at me, as well as Francis's, who was grinning evilly. It seemed, in fact, that both Fortescues were smiling at me with know-it-all expressions.

What a perfect opportunity to talk to Kevin this could

have been, I realized with dismay. Francis's reflection in the window was not only girlish but completely uncool; he was wearing a bowtie, his pants were too short, and his hair which was also too short stuck straight up in a curl at the back of his head. A real mama's boy, I thought. I saw myself the way I imagined Kevin perceived me and my heart sank to my shoes.

"Don't you know that boy, Channe?" Francis said loudly. "Why don't you say hello if you know each other?"

He was right, of course; I was not dealing with the situation in a proper manner. But by now my voice and sensibilities had completely abandoned me.

During *Madame Butterfly* all I could think about was the horrendous, accidental encounter in the subway. It was the first time I truly realized how odd Francis seemed to others, and that our relationship had come to fit into a space and time that I wanted separate from my daily social life. He embarrassed me the same way Candida embarrassed me. They were a constant reminder that I *was* overprotected, childish, and naive when all I wanted was to be sophisticated and adult.

I realized with a terrible, crushing feeling that the reason I did not want Francis to sleep over anymore was that he still pretended we were sexless children; he was holding me back from growing up. I was seized by a terrible, choking rage. All I wanted was to escape.

We had ham sandwiches at a café after the opera, and I was so morose I couldn't speak at all. Francis tapped me gently on the arm and said, "Oh, come now. It's all right. He's so stupid he'll forget by tomorrow that he saw you with me."

Mrs. Fortescue laughed in her shrill, impish way.

What's wrong with this woman, I thought; can't she see that her son is weird?

On the last day of school before summer vacation, Francis announced to me that he was planning to leave École Internationale Bilingue to attend a lycée in the fall. He told me this as we were climbing the back stairway to my apartment. The stairwell was old, musty, and dark. The automatic timer on the lights went out before we'd reached the doorstoop.

"What?" I said, spinning around in the darkness and pressing the light switch again. Francis appeared a few feet before me, leaning his hip against the wooden banister with his arms crossed over his chest.

"I'm tired of it," he said in a defeated tone. He'd developed quite a downy black moustache by then, but hadn't taken to shaving yet.

I was frightened for a moment at the thought of being without him in the fall, but in the next moment I felt immensely relieved. He must have seen this on my face.

"I want to tell you something," he said and took a step toward me. "Now, don't get upset and throw a fit. I know you and I know you're going to throw a fit anyway." He paused, giving me time to imagine every horrible thing in the world. His fingers were lightly tapping his biceps, like fingers practicing piano keys.

"I'm in love with you a little bit," he said. He lifted his right hand off his arm and made a little pinch with his thumb and index finger. "Just a little bit," he said. "It used to be much worse a few years ago but now I've got it under control. And I'm frightfully jealous of all those boys you like. And I'm tired of pretending I don't care."

"You're crazy, Francis," I mumbled, and shook my head, because I did not know what else to do.

He shrugged, as though bored, then turned and went back down the stairs. He'd never intended to come in at all.

The lights went out again and I stood in the darkness. He's lying, I thought, he's just trying to make me mad. But I felt invaded; he'd taken advantage of me, pretended to be my friend and gotten to sleep at the foot of my bed. He'd entered my father's castle in a way no boy had ever done and probably never would again.

But, even if that were true, he was still the best friend I'd ever had. Why say such a thing to me now? Why burn bridges?

During the next few days, as my family packed up to leave for the summer, I vacillated between missing him and hating him.

Finally, I told my father, because, after all, he would probably be able to explain what Francis had meant. My father gazed at me steadily and said, "Poor Francis." I began to feel choked up.

"I hate him," I managed to say.

"No, no. You mustn't be angry," my father said. "He probably meant it. He just didn't know how to say it all along. The only way he could get close to you was by being your best friend. Poor guy."

The next day, we left for Normandie. It took only a few days in a new environment for Francis to move into storage in my mind.

Upon my return in September, I did not call him and he never called me. During the next several years I would run into Francis every now and then on the Rue des Deux Ponts. He was usually with a friend, different boys. At a loss for words, I would ask him if he still played the violin, and he'd vaguely say no, that he'd given it up ages ago. His friends seemed impatient to get him away from me. I supposed it was because people never like to be interrupted by a third party in the street, especially when the mutual friend, in embarrassment or as a simple oversight, fails to introduce the two strangers.

CANDIDA

Often, when I was little, I'd sit quietly, perched on the edge of the kitchen counter while Candida cooked, or cross-legged on a little rug beside her as she shined our shoes, or sometimes straddling the wide end of the ironing board, and listen to her talk. Nothing comforted me more than the sound of her sad and gentle voice and the sharp smells of household chores.

It seemed to me that Candida and I were bonded forever, that we were in life together for the long haul, against the rest of the world. The rest of the world included my parents and Billy.

It may be that I felt bound to Candida because she never disagreed with me or crossed me. And she was like a child herself, living under my father's financial protection and his laws. She loved and feared my father, who was a strong and equable man with a fierce and unpredictable temper. But she forgave him this the way she forgave God for earth-quakes, thunderstorms, and the misery of the world, for she believed that my father had rescued her from what would have been an unhappy life.

Candida was twenty-five when she came to us. She had left Portugal to become a nanny in Paris because the farm near the town of Porto, where she'd spent all her life with her mother, had finally become unmanageable, a lost prop-osition. Before that, she'd never traveled farther from home than the three hundred kilometers to Lisbon.

When Candida talked to me about her own father, she called him "that no-good *filho da puta*." Her mother, Castelha, had never tired of telling Candida about the night her father had run off like a thief, with Castelha's dowry and inheritance and all the jewelry and cash in the house. Candida had been a girl of twelve when this had happened.

"We used to be rich. We used to have a good life," she'd tell me one day, and the next day, forgetting, she'd tell me that her mother liked to exaggerate. Candida did not remember life before her father had left as easy or comfortable at all. There had been a few more cows, chickens, sheep, and goats on the farm, and several men to help, but altogether the men, especially her father, had been cruel and violent and lazy. Candida and her brother and sister had to work after school and on Saturdays until dark.

Candida had a recurring nightmare: Her father, brandishing a thick rope, is chasing a baby goat around the inside of the house. The baby goat runs to Candida who is in the kitchen—tries to hide behind her with its tail between its legs. "No, no, *Pai*!" she cries as her father shoves her out of the way. The baby goat makes it under the table but her father gets down on his hands and knees, swearing, and catches it. Then he cuts its throat.

"But it's only a dream, right, Didi?" I said in a worried and shaky voice when she first told me this. She wouldn't look up from her ironing. Her face was flushed pink, the air filled with the crisp baked-cotton smell of laundered sheets. It was miraculous how close to my knees the iron came and never touched, carried by her swift and certain hand.

"You're right," she said, and shrugged. "It is only a bad dream."

Candida's younger brother and sister had grown tired of the endless work (it seems Castelha could not control them as she could Candida); they had left without glancing back as soon as they were old enough. The brother went to Brazil, and the sister married an English sailor. Neither sent money home and their letters were infrequent, which Candida resented more than the fact that they had left.

Castelha, letting out a tight little sigh, would tell Candida flatly and with finality that she was not surprised to be forgotten by her own rotten children. "You forget those two," she'd say. "They inherited the temperament of their father. You, Candida, you are the only decent child I had from that no-good *filho da puta*. You love this big old sack of potatoes. You don't run away from trouble and hard work."

"They didn't mean any harm to us, *Mae*," Candida would respond in a soothing tone, feeling pious and enjoying the compliment, although she did not like for her mother to talk of them as though they were dead. It was bad luck.

"And I'm going to die young, working like this and no one will care but you."

Finally, when the farm had to be sold, commiserating friends and neighbors told Castelha that Candida should go to Paris. They had relatives who had gone, who wrote home that there was good money to be made, and even enclosed money orders in their letters.

It took a good deal of persuading, but Castelha finally agreed that there was no other solution. Candida wrote to the neighbors' relatives and a position was found for her in a proper French family.

The farm was sold and Castelha managed to pay off most of her debts. She moved to Porto and began to sew for a living. She was an extraordinary seamstress and had secretly always wanted to make a living that way. Castelha herself told me this five years later, when she came to Paris to pay us a visit, and made me the most perfect red velvet party dress with a white lace collar and cuffs and a white satin ribbon at the waist. I watched this miraculous enterprise for three days, while she babbled away in a mix of Portuguese and French, in the happiest of moods.

"Sewing makes me happy," she told me, "like nothing else in the world." She was a short, round woman who somehow did not seem flabby. Maybe she wore some tight girdle that kept her all pulled tight. She reminded me of a big rock.

Her voice went maudlin and she added, "I miss my Candida terribly in Porto."

I didn't like this comment one bit: Every moment

Castelha was with us I feared that she'd take Candida away with her at the end of her stay.

"She's my Candida as much as yours," I said to Castelha in a little hard voice, which made her laugh heartily.

Candida's first three months in Paris were unhappy ones. The French *patrons* reprimanded her the first time she took an orange from the refrigerator without asking and she never did it again. Every week they withdrew money from her paycheck for food and for her train ride from Portugal, and half of the rest she sent to her mother with joyful, enthusiastic notes, because she did not want her mother to worry.

The French *patrons'* two children were sweet and well-behaved, but they did not seem to need her and she felt no warmth from them. This bothered her most.

Her room was a tiny garret on the top floor of the apartment building on fancy Avenue Foche. She spent a good deal of time in her room, sitting and thinking. She told me once, when I was a bit older, that she had not minded being unhappy because she believed that all forms of human suffering were God's tests, and therefore good for the character, and that the better you behaved under duress, the better you'd be rewarded later on.

When I repeated this to my father (I was about eight at the time), he winced uncomfortably and suddenly turned quite crimson.

"And that's exactly why I hate priests!" he cried out. "They're liars and hypocrites, they use religion to keep poor peasants like Candida under control!" His voice grew louder as he spoke until he was finally shouting at the space before his nose. "They tell them, 'Be patient, it's better in heaven!' While they, the goddamn pious PRICKS, LIVE LIKE KINGS OFF THE MONEY OF THE RICH!"

I sat there, stunned, while he thought in silence for a moment. You could never be sure what would throw him into a fury. Some things just hit him the wrong way. It was disconcerting, and everyone was terrified of his fits. Sometimes he broke things, or punched a wall.

"But don't tell Candida I said that," he added, his voice suddenly gentle. "You'll just upset her."

I kept my mouth shut and had my first seriously ambivalent thought. Who was right? My father, I knew, was smarter than Candida, and did not lie, although he sometimes confused what he'd written in a book with reality.

Candida, as far as I knew, never lied either. So who was right?

Candida had arrived in Paris with the phone number of one young woman from Porto she knew personally, a girl she'd gone to school with who'd had a bad reputation. There had been rumors of flirtations that had gone too far, of a rich landowner showering her with gifts—Candida paid little attention to such things. The girl's uncle had slipped Candida the phone number when Castelha was not looking; Candida had slipped it into her pocket without saying a word.

At first she avoided calling Maria but loneliness finally led her to a pay phone one Sunday afternoon. Maria sounded thrilled to hear from her and immediately offered to come fetch her. She told Candida to wait right outside the cafe.

"Now, for God's sake don't smile at any men or they'll think you're a prostitute!" Maria said, laughing shrilly into the phone. Candida's heart almost stopped; she'd never heard a girl talk that way. By the time I was six, however, she called a *maricon* a maricon and a *puta* a puta.

Although Candida did not listen to gossip, she felt safer not mentioning Maria in her letters home—in Portugal, to avoid trouble, Candida would have passed Maria in the street with only a slight nod of recognition. The news of the budding friendship would have thrown Castelha into one of her attacks of high blood pressure, in which her face became blotchy and her breaths short and she collapsed prostrate on the closest couch or bed.

Candida felt guilty, but her Sunday afternoon in Maria's *patron*'s kitchen was the only fun she had all week. Maria was a ray of sunshine; she dressed nicely, brightly, wore makeup (maybe too much), laughed all the time, smoked cigarettes, and served Porto wine in tiny stemmed crystal glasses, and *chourico* with bread on a pretty blue plate.

Maria tried to coax Candida into going out with her and two Portuguese boys she knew but Candida only wanted to sit in the kitchen and talk about home. Maria was working for an American businessman whose apartment was on Place des Vosges. Maria told Candida, who cried quietly but often about her French *patrons*, that she should go to work for an American. They weren't as cheap, Maria said, they weren't as unpleasant, they never noticed if things were clean or not, and they treated their maids like human beings and not slaves or dogs.

"But I couldn't work for an unmarried man. My mother would be horrified," Candida pointed out.

"You're so funny," Maria said. "And how's your mother going to know who you're working for?"

"Someone would write to her and tell her," Candida said, as though to report were simply every person's moral obligation.

"You're so funny. Can't you see that you're in Paris now?" Maria chided her.

Maria took it upon herself to get Candida out of her bad situation. She approached her American businessman on Candida's behalf. "This girl from my hometown," Maria said in all earnestness, "is like a saint. A saint, I tell you! I would leave her alone in a room with a million francs."

A few days after this conversation, the businessman gave Maria the phone number of a young American couple who were in immediate need of a nanny—my parents.

The following Sunday, Maria pressed the number into Candida's palm. She repeated what the businessman had told her: The Willises were a young American couple—the husband was a writer, they had just had a baby—and they were looking for a full-time nanny.

"Call them," Maria insisted. "You drive me crazy, Candida," she said exasperatedly. "What good is life if you don't take advantage of it?"

* * *

My parents asked Candida to come by right away, explaining that they had had a good deal of trouble with their domestics and were now quite desperate. This was not an exaggeration. They'd been in Paris less than a year, a newlywed couple with no clear notion of how to run a household, and their first attempt at domestics had landed them a Sikh and his Liverpudlian wife, jewel thieves hiding from Interpol. The Sikh carried a switchblade and the wife wore gold, high-heeled mules and her hair in a bright red bouffant. My parents found them a bit garish for European domestics, but hadn't had any domestics before with whom to compare them.

The relationship had ended in a switchblade confrontation between my father and the Sikh.

Calling the domestics out of the kitchen after dinner one evening, my father explained very calmly, apologetically, that although he found the Sikh a terrific cook, his rough manner and condescending glares were inappropriate while serving dinner, especially to guests.

"And your wife," my father went on, "likes to burn holes with the iron in my wife's dresses."

There was no reaction whatsoever.

"You seem very unhappy," my father concluded. "This work doesn't seem cut out for you. We believe you'd be much better off doing something else."

In an action so quick that my pregnant mother saw only a flicker in her peripheral vision, the Sikh lunged at my father and stuck his switchblade under his chin. Holding the knife in a shaky hand, he said in a blood-chilling, hate-filled voice, "You think you're some hot stuff, don't you?"

My father, who'd been somewhat expecting a confrontation, leapt out of his chair, grabbed the man's wrist with his left hand, pinned him down on the dining-room table sending the dishes flying, and stuck his own switchblade under the Sikh's chin.

My father had carried a switchblade himself ever since he'd been in combat in the Pacific, and slept with a pistol under the bed. This was antithetical to his adamantly pacifist views, but had become a habit he could not break, and never did break for the rest of his life.

The Sikh's eyes went round and white while my father glared down at him with an evil grin.

"I've killed a man in hand-to-hand combat before so don't think for a second I won't do it," he said slowly. "I'll give you ten minutes to pack up and get out of my house; after that I'm calling the police."

The Sikh's wife, as a last statement, came up from behind and knocked my mother's plate off the table and the leftover lamb Vindaloo landed on her lap.

"You nouveau-riche Americans make me sick," said the Sikh's wife, and spat on the floor.

"And you're just a dumb, low-class slut with no taste," my mother said calmly, picking up the chunks of lamb and putting them back on her plate.

The Sikh's wife screamed and ran from the dining room.

In ten minutes they were gone and not a trace of them was left in the little room they had occupied at the bottom of the back stairway.

A week later a detective came by with a warrant for the Sikh and his wife's arrest and the whole truth came out.

My parents remained without live-in domestics until I was born, at which time they hired a large-chested, pie-faced Bavarian widow. Although terribly good-natured, Fräu Hausler liked her Kronenbourg and after three or four bottles, spoke nostalgically of life under the Third Reich. She would sing "Deutchland, Deutchland Über Alles" to me in a booming voice and then cry, telling my parents that she had nothing against Americans because, after all, real Americans were mostly Aryan like the Germans, but how much better off the world would have been had the Nazis won the War. Finally my father got into an argument with Fräu Hausler on this subject and fired her on the spot.

As soon as Candida walked into our apartment with her frightened, wide-open, angular face and her halo of black kinky hair, my parents fell in love with her. She sat down in a corner of the sofa holding her cheap little bag on her knees. Her hands were strong and pink and her legs, beneath the stockings, were black and hairy.

In timid, halting French, Candida explained her situation. She told them about the farm's misfortune, that sudden poverty had scattered her family across the world. She told about the French couple who had brought her from Portugal and treated their dog with more respect than they did her.

My father thought that her story sounded quite a bit like the Sikh's, and like Fräu Hausler's as well, and gathered that all domestics had a touch of the Cinderella syndrome and that it was a completely forgivable trait.

"The dog they think will not steal," Candida said, "but I know that dog and that dog will steal off the table while for me to take an orange is a terrible thing."

My parents enthusiastically explained, also in halting French, that they'd just had their first baby, a girl who was now two months old. Candida asked to see the child. They took her downstairs to the nursery and all three stood around my crib in silence, peering down at me as though I were some rare and fragile object that needed to be kept under glass.

My parents were nervous around me. It had been a very difficult pregnancy for my mother. Her water had broken at six months and she'd had to lie still, on heavy medication, until the delivery. My father had moved his typewriter into the room next door, had brought her meals to the bed, had cleaned her, brought her bed pot to her, and had never left her side although he was a person who loved to sit in bars and restaurants until they closed, talking to strangers and friends alike about the state of the world. Instead, my father brought the party to their bedroom, and friends would gather around and drink and tell jokes and keep my mother in a good mood.

After the high-forceps delivery, the doctors told my mother that the chances of her ever having another child were not good.

Driving us home from the American hospital in Neuilly in his little white convertible Mercedes Benz, my father had refused to exceed twenty miles an hour. My mother sat with me in the tiny back seat, yelling over my father's shoulder that they were going to have an accident if he didn't speed up. Cars honked, drivers shouted at them and swung their fists, but my father, wiping large drops of sweat off his forehead with the back of his hand, would not accelerate.

They were still absolutely petrified around me and in the week since Fräu Hausler's departure, had taken to hiring a registered nurse to come give me a bath because they were terrified of drowning me.

"May I?" Candida gestured toward my crib. My parents nodded nervously, and Candida slowly, gently lifted me out, one hand beneath the neck and head and one around the tiny body. She cooed and mumbled in Portuguese, and rocked me against her chest. I was born with black black hair, like a Mexican, and one thin lock stuck straight up above the forehead. Candida decided she would put a little bow there, a little pink one, if God were kind enough to offer her this charge.

She said, "She look like a little Mexican baby."

"There's American Indian blood on Monsieur's side," my mother said, smiling with profound relief at Candida.

"When she was born," my father put in, "I said, 'I know who the father is but who's the mother?'" He chuckled loudly and Candida stared at him, missing the joke.

"But this hair fall out," Candida said reassuringly. "With blue eyes maybe later she be blond like you, Madame. I raised from infants my brother and sister." She laughed lightly. "I was not much more than an infant myself."

She put me back in the crib and then her face tragically collapsed.

"Ay, what nice peoples you are. And I am so unhappy with those French. I still owe them much money for the trip from Portugal."

"How much do you still owe them?" my mother asked.

Candida shrugged. "Maybe a hundred and fifty, maybe two hundred francs."

My father took out his wallet and started counting out bills.

"Here's three hundred francs."

"No, no, I couldn't."

"You take it," my mother said. "Tell them you are

coming here tomorrow. If there is a problem, my husband will talk to them."

The next afternoon Candida arrived with a suitcase, a wicker basket, and a face flushed pink with pleasure. She gave my father back a hundred and seventy-five francs, explaining that they'd only asked for a hundred and twenty-five.

"Cheap French bastards," my father said, horrified that they would actually hold a penniless person accountable for such a measly sum. He was so thrilled by her honesty that he told her to keep the money. He pushed the bills toward her with a flat, downward motion of his hand.

"I'll send it to my mother in Porto," she said, clasping the bills to her chest.

Candida's room was right next to the nursery. It was an all-purpose room with a blue linoleum floor, a sink, and a small, plastic rectangle of a shower. There was a single bed against one wall and a colorful rug below it. She asked if she could take a few francs out of the house budget for plants, and my parents immediately agreed. They told her to take as much money as she needed to fix the room up the way she wanted it. This confused her slightly, as it was a big room and Candida had simple tastes.

On the wall above her bed she hung a few religious watercolors in ornate, gold frames. One, in soft, earthy colors, depicted Christ giving the Sermon on the Mount, another was of the Crucifixion and in it Christ's eyes moved, following you around the room with the changing light, and the last was of Saint Bernadette of Lourdes kneeling before the apparition of the Immaculate Conception. This one was all rosy and the sun streaked through a cloudy sky in brilliant white lines. These had hung in her bedroom all her life; she had brought them with her from Portugal.

With her first paycheck she bought a little porcelain statue of the Virgin Mary with robes painted blue, her arms outstretched in an embrace to the world, and placed her on the windowsill at the head of the bed. These objects made her feel protected and safe. And I, her new charge, was suddenly so entirely in her care that Candida felt God had reversed his orders regarding her life, and had chosen to bestow on her a providential gift.

When I was two, we went to Haiti for the winter; my father was gathering research for a book. Our house was on the beach; the sea practically came up to our front porch. Candida could not swim, but pushed me around in a rubber life preserver in front of the house, in water that came up to her chest. My father could watch us from the window of the study where he wrote. One morning he heard a horrendous scream and looking up, saw terrific splashing and arms flailing the water. He knocked his chair over running for the door. He saw that Candida was fighting something in the water, and trying to hoist me onto her shoulder at the same time. I was emitting a gurgling sound so filled with terror and pain that it made my father's blood freeze. Then he saw the bluish bladderlike sac of the floating Portuguese man-of-war, and its oozing tentacles wrapped around Candida's body and the lower part of my legs. Even in her panic, her eyes white with fear and shock, Candida refused to let go of me. My father threw himself into the water and pulled us out.

Candida was much more badly stung than I, so badly in fact, that she contracted a high fever and was bedridden for days.

"What kind of a thing was that thing? A thing from the Devil it was," she said to my father.

"A Portuguese man-o-war," he said. "A jellyfish."

"How could a Portuguese thing do that to another Portuguese?" Candida said, her dark eyes spilling tears.

This nearly disastrous event shook my father so completely that he told the story for years. "She would have drowned, I swear to you, before she'd have let you go. I never saw a person show more devotion to a child that wasn't her own."

Candida and I spoke our own form of childish French, with English and Portuguese mixed in. So many Portuguese words had invaded my vocabulary that even my parents had started to use them. *Passarinho*—a birdie—"When you sit, don't spread your legs like that, Channe," my parents would say. "People can see your *pass.*"

By three, I'd developed insomnia. But my neurosis was limited to Saturday and Sunday nights. Saturday's insomnia was in preparation for Sunday's—the only night of the week I was separated from Candida.

I waited until my parents had gone out before I cried in my bed on Saturdays. Candida tried to avoid running to me because my father had warned her not to. But from her room next door, she could hear my whimpering and sobbing as it grew progressively louder. When she could no longer bear it, she came running to me. She 'd appear in the doorway in a white nightgown, translucent with the light behind her.

Candida's arrival would throw me into an even more violent fit of emotion. I'd stop breathing, or begin to choke on my tears—and Candida would sit on the bed and take me in her arms.

When I'd calmed down a little, I'd ask, "Where do you go tomorrow? Who do you love more than me?" in a hard voice heavy with resentment and jealousy.

Candida would shrug unhappily and explain that it was not her choice: My parents *made* her leave on Sundays. It occurred to me several years later that this was not entirely so—Candida liked her day off as much as most working people do.

"Take me with you to Maria's," I'd say.

"Your papa and mama wants to be with you on Sundays."

"Then why do they always have a party on Sunday night?"

She'd shrug, making a tight-lipped pious face, as though to say she disagreed with their parenting but did not have a say in my upbringing.

My parents had a poker game on Sunday nights. It had started one Sunday because they'd had to babysit me, and had bled into the next, and the next. It had become a tradition in our house. Any American in Paris who wanted a good plate of spaghetti bolognese (it was the only dish my mother could make but she made it extraordinarily well) and a good poker game, came to our house on Sunday night. Sometimes we'd find them still there on Monday morning, stooped around the green felt table, pungent glasses and ashtrays at their elbows and clouds of smoke around their heads.

"I don't know why," Candida would tell me. "They don't care about you like I do, I suppose. I been feeding you and changing you and staying with you late at night since the night the President Kennedy was elected and you mama drank too much champagne."

"One day you're going to get married and leave me."

"Never."

"If you ever get married, will you live with us with your husband and children?"

She'd laugh, throwing back her head, her face crimson.

"Stay here with me to sleep," I'd beg, wrapping my arms like a vise around her neck.

"I can't." She'd try to pull me off. "You papa say no. You know how he get mad." I'd beg and whine until she finally conceded, and promised to spend the night with me.

With the good intention of waiting for me to fall asleep, Candida would stretch out beside me and pretend to go to sleep. I also waited, knowing that if I fell asleep first, Candida would leave. It was a battle of wills that I sometimes won and sometimes lost.

If Candida managed to leave the room and I awoke, the crying and wailing started again immediately. And then when she'd come running to me, I'd attack her for betraying me:

"You lied to me! You lied! You left!"

But once in a while, Candida nodded off first. In my victory, I instantly found sleep, imagining I was floating above the city, enveloped in a cloud.

Sundays were wonderful days. My parents took me to the park or to the movies. Sometimes we went to the Zoo de Vincennes with Lyddie Lowenstein, a collagist who was divorced and had no children. She was always stopping on the walkways and picking up bits of discarded paper—a candy wrapper, a cigarette butt that struck her the right way, or a peanut shell with a peculiar shape.

"You always find the most interesting things at the zoo," Lyddie would say.

There was an American Buffalo at the Zoo de Vincennes, and Lyddie liked to lean over the cement ledge and yell at it, "Yankee go home!," which made my parents roar with laughter. The French people threw nasty glances in our direction.

"We'll make an American out of you yet," Lyddie would tell me.

It was only with the coming of night that the panic and the gloom set in, when the sun went down and the guests started to arrive and Candida didn't come back.

The more voices I heard crowding into the living room up the short flight of stairs from my room, the worse it would become.

My parents had no idea how seriously I took my Sunday night trauma.

"Mommy," I'd say at bedtime in a worried voice, "I think I'm not going to be able to sleep."

"You just miss Didi," she'd respond offhandedly. It was the nature of my mother to be lackadaisical, disorganized, and light-hearted. I wanted her to take me seriously but nothing I could say or do, short of really hurting myself, worked.

She'd ask offhandedly, "Did you brush your teeth?"

"Yes."

"Good girl. It's very important to brush your teeth."

I never brushed my teeth. Later, it was the same with homework.

"Did you do your homework?"

"Yes."

"Good."

There was no such thing as negative reinforcement in my family. If, for attention, I responded, "No, I didn't do my homework," her reaction was also indifferent. "Well, don't you think it's about time you did?" she'd say, and immediately move on to something else, while she sent me off to my room.

"You want to be thrown to the sharks tonight?" she'd ask me on Sunday night, since my parents were the ones who put me to bed.

"Oh *yes!*"

My mother clasped my hands and my father my feet, and they swung me, One, Two, Three, into my big double bed. This was called throwing Channe to the sharks, and although it only lasted a moment, it was a most exciting event.

"If you can't sleep don't worry about it. Look at a book. If you *really* can't sleep, come upstairs and lie on the couch," my mother said.

Which I invariably did, dragging my blanket behind me. I waited a few hours, which was the appropriate amount of time. Anything short of that would have angered my parents.

The grown-ups looked on in glassy-eyed wonderment. "Is this healthy?" they'd whisper. "Are you sure you shouldn't send her back to bed?"

"What the hell?" I'd hear my father say. "She'll fall asleep on the couch in two minutes."

Later in the night, he'd carry me back to my bed.

My parents worried, but not excessively, about this bad habit of mine. It was as I grew older and continued these Saturday night tantrums that they began to show real concern. Meanwhile, my brother Billy had fallen quite naturally into the rhythm of our lives. Now we had two of everything, but only one Candida, whom I would not share with him.

I turned seven, eight, nine, and still could not sleep on Sunday nights. My parents had hoped that Billy's presence would alleviate my feelings of loneliness and my attachment to Candida, but he only turned me into a jealous, raving lunatic. My mother had taken to favoring Billy because I seemed stronger on the outside, more outspoken, more controlling—and I had Candida on my side, who protected me fiercely against him. I had come to cling to Candida in an even more desperate way.

At ten, I was still sucking my thumb and throwing tantrums on Saturday nights. My father, checking in on Billy and me one night, found Candida asleep in my bed. His rage was so enormous it engulfed the room like a sudden fire.

Candida awakened terrified. My father had thrown the covers back and was pulling her out of my bed by both arms. With curses and brandishing fists, he chased her from my room into her own. She locked herself in while my father kicked and pounded on the door.

"DON'T YOU UNDERSTAND THAT YOU'RE MAKING A MESS OF HER? I'M SICK OF IT! YOU'RE FIRED!"

"Bill—" I heard my mother mumble behind him. I had barely noticed her before that; she'd faded completely in the presence of my father's wrath.

"YOU SHUT UP! AND *YOU*!" He kicked Candida's door, "I WANT YOU OUT OF HERE BY THE CRACK OF DAWN! DO YOU HEAR ME? NO MORE FUCKING AROUND!"

Once he'd stormed off, my mother in tow, I tiptoed to Candida's door and knocked, crying out in a tiny voice, "Didi! Didi! Let me in!"

Candida was sobbing, too frightened to move.

Suddenly Billy was standing in the doorway of his room—the old nursery that stood between Candida's room and mine—barefooted, half-asleep, and blinking at me, stupefied.

I hated him at that moment for being so independent, never needing anybody, for being able to sleep anywhere, anytime, as soon as you told him to lie down.

"Go away!" I said, glaring at him. I collapsed in a ball at the foot of Candida's door, and wept. He stood over me for a long time. Finally, I fell asleep. In the morning, Candida found me curled up like a cat on her rubber welcome mat.

She immediately began to pack her bags.

"But where are you going to go?" I asked, wringing my hands. I was trying to think fast—what could I say to my father to convince him to change his mind?

She shed the largest tears I'd ever seen; they were like clear marbles rolling from her eyes. Her face was set, and she was biting her lips so that her mouth twisted downward in one thin curving line.

She packed all the gifts my mother had given her—the shoes, the fancy Italian handbag, the wool sweaters. At the bottom of her suitcase she'd laid out all my chefs d'oeuvre from art class, categorized by year.

My father was just waking up about then. More than a little hungover, he couldn't remember exactly what had been said. He put on a robe and came down to the back of the apartment.

He stood in Candida's doorway for a moment. I glared at him, paralyzed with hatred. He cleared his throat and sheepishly offered her another chance. He insisted that he had not intended to be cruel—although he knew we both thought so—but that my well-being was at stake.

"She's not growing up normally because she's too attached to you," he said regretfully. "And you're the grown-up here. You have to take responsibility. Channe, leave us alone, will you?"

I left the room. I couldn't understand what he was talking about and at that moment found him to be the cruelest, most awful, most unloving person in the world.

"There won't be a next time, Didi," I heard him say as I closed the door, his voice grave and sad.

I only recall one further occasion in which Candida fell asleep in my bed. It was a spring night, and a terrible lightning storm swept through the city. My mother, presumably to avoid another explosion, alone came to check on us when my parents got home.

"*Vite!*" I heard her whisper as she shook Candida awake. "*Vite*, go back to your own room before Monsieur finds out!"

Candida left in a hurry, mumbling, "*Merci, Madame,*" in an apologetic, confused way.

My mother sat down beside me.

"I don't know what to tell you, Channe," she said, shaking her head.

"Stay with me till I fall asleep," I asked, without much hope.

"I'll stay for a little while. Your daddy's waiting for me." After a moment, she added, "If he catches her in here again he's going to send her back to Portugal. Don't you understand that? What's wrong with you?" She sounded worried, the way she did when I had a fever.

"It was the storm," I said flatly. "We were scared."

"She's just a little girl," my mother said to herself. And turning to me, said, "Just like you."

Soon after that, Candida developed an allergy that made her eyes swell up so that she couldn't open them. The family doctor tested her for everything by giving her little shots in the forearm. The only elements her skin reacted to were feathers and dust, and the reactions were in no way compatible with the swelling of her eyes. The doctor told her the allergy appeared to be psychosomatic, and suggested she find another, less trying line of work. Candida told him that this was simply impossible and would not hear another word. She began to sleep with icepacks over her eyes and stuff her pillows with synthetic sponge instead of feathers.

Then, while cleaning a shelf, she smashed a magnificent Roman amphora my father had brought up from the sea on a scubadiving expedition. She cried bitterly over her clumsiness. She had hit the amphora with her hip, she told us, and it had slipped off the shelf and shattered on the floor.

Candida hid in the kitchen, weeping and wringing her hands in a dish towel, while in the dining room Billy and I sat quietly and watched our father try to put the amphora back together. He had laid the jagged, ancient, sea-bleached pieces of clay out on a newspaper, and was sitting at the head of the table, staring at them with a hopeless look.

"See these tiny worms?" he asked us, holding up a large fragment. The worms looked like bloodless veins on the smooth, beige surface. "These worms are so so old the sea turned them into part of the clay." He said this without emotion, although a tear, which he ignored, dropped out of his eye.

"You know what I believe? I believe people do things

subconsciously on purpose. Like when people get hit by a car when life's not going their way. Now, Didi knew how much this meant to me. Diving for it, bringing it up; it's part of my being a man and all that kind of crap, but I was damn proud of this thing.

"It's irreplaceable," he added flatly. "But I'm just not going to get upset."

"Didi's real upset, Daddy," I said quickly.

"I know. I know she is. But I'll tell you something. She thinks her life is hard because of me. She doesn't have control of things the way most grown-ups do. See, I make all the decisions around here.

"She didn't *mean* to bump the shelf; but just maybe she was unconsciously careless.

"Oh hell," he said, getting up with a big sigh. He crumpled the newspaper in a swift sweeping gesture, walked over to the closest wastepaper basket, shoved the whole thing in, and stepped on it with his foot.

Billy and I found a wounded sparrow stuck under the old, heavy wooden door that was the back entrance to our apartment building. We were probably ten or eleven.

"It must have gotten scared and flew right into the door trying to get out," Billy said in a sorrowful voice. It took all of his patience and cool-headedness to get the sparrow out without wounding it further. I stood behind him, jumping up and down and screaming as he lay stomach down on the sidewalk with his hands under the door. Billy directed me to go fetch a shoe box upstairs.

"Put some cotton in it," he said. "Hurry up!"

I grumbled a good deal, but returned with the box. Billy held the tiny bird in his cupped hands and gently deposited it in the cotton. It wouldn't lie still; it banged into the sides, trying to get out.

"It has a broken wing," Billy said thoughtfully. "But maybe it'll get fixed if it'll sit still for a while. Maybe we can take it to the *vétérinaire*?"

"What are you, crazy? You think they're going to let us take it to the *vétérinaire*?"

"Well, I'm keeping it," he said with finality, which was his way with everything, once his mind was set.

"You're a jerk," I told him, disgusted.

Candida did not like the bird one bit. If it had been my bird she would have been more compliant. She insisted that the bird wasn't going to live two days in that box. She said our mom's cats would get it for sure.

I went against Billy for the hell of it, and because the sick bird gave me ammunition with which to abuse him. I didn't really care one way or the other about the bird. The issue became a battle of wills—his against mine and Candida's. As the bird grew weaker, continuing its miserable attempts to fly out of the box, I reveled in the fact that he was wrong and we were right.

But Billy stubbornly and silently ignored me and Candida. He went straight to our father, who was the boss (and considerably less squeamish than our mother or Candida about street animals), and got permission to keep the sparrow, at least for a few more days.

Billy put the box high up on a shelf in his closet, where the cats couldn't climb.

After two days, the bird still would not eat and still tried to fly out of the box, bashing its wings against the sides. It made a horrible, skittering sound that attracted the cats, who sat patiently in front of Billy's closet, waiting. Billy finally kicked the cats in the behind, and hissed them out of his room.

"How dare you kick the cats!" I said, full of self-righteousness. Ten minutes later they were back, having come through from my room to his, through the archway that had no door.

Exasperated, I told Candida to go talk to our father. She went to him on the third day and told him that Billy was torturing the bird. She said it was clearly dying and he was just prolonging its misery. Our father did not like things to take a long time to die and told Candida to get rid of it quickly and without any hoopla.

It must have been a Saturday because my bedroom seemed particularly bright and sunny, not long with shadows like a late, after-school afternoon. Billy and I were arguing over GI Joe's jeep—Barbie wanted to take it for a spin but GI Joe wasn't in the mood to comply—when Candida suddenly walked through holding something between her hands, at arm's length. It was the sparrow, twirling round and round in frantic, quivering pirouettes.

Candida had pierced it through the eyes with a long sewing needle. She was holding the pin horizontally at both ends while the sparrow spun round and round the pin. Her pale, angular face displayed no emotion, neither pleasure nor horror, just a flatness, which horrified me.

Billy and I stood up at once, staring at the poor, blinded sparrow.

"It was dying, *pobrecito*," Candida said in a toneless voice. "I'm putting it out of its misery."

Billy backed away from the sight, turned completely white. He headed for the bathroom in slow-motion, stiff like a sleepwalker. I found him kneeling around the toilet with his face in the bowl.

For days the sight of food made him blanch and he would not eat.

"The bird was dying, Billy," our father said sadly, in a soft earnest tone. He had no idea, and Billy never said one word about what we'd seen.

The memory left a terrible itch in my lower abdomen, like a hand tickling me from the inside. I felt Candida had betrayed me, although I knew I was to blame—and for a long time I could not look her in the eyes.

Candida met Mamadou about a year later, on the way to the market. He was the manservant and chauffeur of our new neighbor, a high-ranking diplomat who'd spent years in the Belgian Congo.

It took Mamadou three months to work up the nerve to ask Candida if he could help her carry her groceries back to our house. Then they began to go to church together on Sundays. Mamadou was as religious as Candida; he'd been converted by a zealous Catholic missionary who'd taught him to read and write in French.

Six months passed before Mamadou formally asked her out. He'd asked his *patron*'s permission to take Candida for a spin in the black Citroen with government plates. It was spring and they packed a picnic. They went all the way to Fontainebleau before they stopped to eat at a picnic area that had wooden tables and benches under large chestnut trees. "I can drive very fast and no policeman will stop me," Mamadou said proudly, "because of the diplomatic plates."

Eventually, Mamadou took to visiting our kitchen. He'd sit and watch while Candida moved swiftly and expertly about the small space. It was immediately apparent to Billy and me that Mamadou was in love. He'd gaze at Candida admiringly, ask her for recipes, as though her cuisine was the most elegant and important thing in the world.

They did not talk much in general. Their conversations were mostly about the weather and the state of affairs in France. Their information came only from the trashy gossip papers, which made them experts on the private lives of the rich and famous—who'd had an abortion and who'd been arrested for drunk driving, for example.

Mamadou was a handsome man. He had extraordinarily delicate features, large eyes that were shockingly black, and shockingly white. His skin was not murky like coffee, but like a polished onyx stone, so black that it gleamed in the light.

Billy and I were fascinated by the palms of his hands and his nails, which were so pink in comparison to the rest of him that they seemed unreal, dyed. His hands were a different black than his face, blue black. We liked to touch his palms and fingertips, at which he laughed complacently.

His attentions caused Candida to blush furiously, leading us to believe she might be a little in love as well. Altogether, we thought, and our parents thought, that it was a perfect match.

After six more months of this very spiritual courtship, Mamadou proposed.

He went to my father first, in his funereal Sunday church suit. On a weekday morning, while Candida was out shopping, he climbed the musty back stairwell of our apartment building to the third floor, which was my father's office.

My father wasn't the least bit surprised. He was, in fact, extremely relieved and pleased. He called my mother on the intercom and told her the good news. Within a few minutes, she joined them.

They immediately began to discuss the arrangements. My father told Mamadou that as a wedding present, he'd buy them the old concierge's apartment on the ground floor which had been empty for some time. He offered to hire Mamadou but said he probably wouldn't be able to pay him as much as the French diplomat did. Mamadou said he'd already talked to his *patron* and that it was decided that he'd still be the diplomat's chauffeur, but no longer his manservant. Instead, he would take on some duties in our house.

My mother put in her two cents. "You know, Mamadou, Candida is like a young girl—"

"I know, Madame." He looked down at the floor.

"All right, that's all I wanted to say," said my mother.

A salary was agreed upon for Mamadou and they all shook hands. My father sent him back downstairs with my mother to wait for Candida.

Candida refused him. No one knows what words passed between them; Candida would never say. That afternoon, a heavy, uncomfortable silence descended on our house and remained for several days. It was as though someone had passed away. Candida, pale and silent, did not cry but attacked her work with a vengeance. She scrubbed behind the refrigerator and under the washing machine, and other such places that had never been cleaned before.

Soon afterward, Mamadou's diplomat was called back into service and they moved away and were never seen again.

I asked her once, some time later, why she'd said no to Mamadou. She shrugged offhandedly and looked away.

I pressed her. "Come on, Didi. You always tell me everything."

"Maria was teasing me," she said in a distant voice. "She said my mother will get a heart attack. Can you imagine? I liked him well. But I didn't want café-au-lait babies."

I told her she was foolish, I told her that her café-au-lait babies would have been beautiful. She shrugged heavily, as though shifting a terrible weight from one shoulder to the other.

I told my father what she'd said. He shook his head and said, "That might be part of it, but that's not really it. She was afraid for other reasons."

Within a year, she was asthmatic. Her shoulders had begun to droop permanently, and her face had lost its rosy color. Her skin was now pasty white and the wrinkles at her eyes and mouth had turned her face hard, unyielding.

Candida had always been relatively open with me about her body—she changed her sanitary napkins in front of me. As soon as I began to menstruate, her attitude changed. An embarrassing silence replaced her joking, light-hearted, shallow talk about "whores" and "maricons" and the love lives of stars. Sex had been fine, in her opinion, as long as it had stayed away from her, and by osmosis, me.

She could no longer bear to have boys visit my bedroom, if only to sit at the table and have a piece of cake. She hovered behind us every moment, disgruntled, watching. The air was heavy with her presence.

In the summer of my twelfth year, my family went to Normandie for two months. Candida went to Portugal to visit her mother. On our first day in Deauville, my father bought me a little red bikini on the boardwalk, and then took me for a stroll down the beach. The Channel was at low tide. We had to walk far on the hard, wet sand to get to the water.

My father took me by the hand, which seemed rather strange now that I was so grown-up. It occurred to me that a whole year had passed since the last time he'd taken my hand and walked with me on a beach, and that he had forgotten how much I'd grown.

"Candida's not coming back," he said carefully, and waited for my reaction. My thoughts were immediately scrambled; I did not know whether to act furious at this subterfuge, or whether to listen. One thing was certain: He was the most trustworthy person I knew, honest to a fault. In his honesty, he was always hardest on himself.

"Why?" I asked.

"Believe me it hurts me terribly, honey," he said. He looked out over the Channel, but turned and focused on me from time to time. "I could barely stand to do it. I sent her home for a year. I felt so goddamn guilty I gave her enough money to buy her mother a house on the beach and retire if she wanted. This is such a crucial time for you. You need space, to be independent.

"You know what's wrong with me? I'm a coward, that's what's wrong with me. I should've done it years ago. But a better, more trustworthy nanny we never would've found. She loves you too much and it's ruining you."

We walked for a long time. The wind was blowing, stinging my face and throwing my hair from side to side.

My father talked about normal love and obsessive love, about Candida's repressed sexuality that had never come to the surface and had turned inward, into allergies and asthma and insomnia. He said she'd funneled all the feeling she should have had for a man into me, and never realized it.

"You can't be someone's passion, someone's whole life, unless you're that person's lover, you see. Someone's husband or wife. And even then, it's dangerous.

"Goddamn it, I wish she'd married Mamadou. What scares me most is that I might have waited too long. That you'll never recover. You're so spoiled, so used to getting your way. I don't want you to be a mess—about sex and otherwise, you know?"

Know? I had only a dim, childish notion of what he was talking about. I certainly did not think I was a mess, compared to all the emotionally wounded, lonely, unhappy kids I knew at school. Well—so oftentimes I couldn't sleep. But I'd finally talked to our family doctor about it and he'd said, So what? Some people can sleep and some people can't. It's your metabolical clock.

We were used to not having Candida with us during summer vacations. She often went home to Portugal while we traveled *en famille*. But vacations stood apart from real life. I did not begin to miss Candida abnormally until we got home, and every night was like a Sunday. Like an addicted person, I began my withdrawal. I wrote her a letter every night, and she wrote me back. Three times a week we talked on the phone. My father permitted this for the first few weeks; he felt responsible, I suppose.

One week into school, I stubbornly announced to my parents that I was going to Portugal by myself for my Easter vacation. I added that Didi was paying for the ticket.

My parents, gazing at me skeptically, said fine, if that was what I wanted to do.

I never went to Portugal. Within six months, being cool and hip at school had become more important to me than my loyalty to Candida. I was reluctant to surrender my new-found freedom to visit her, even for ten days. I made up an excuse—I blamed it on my parents. In a self-indulgent, snivelly letter, I wrote that they thought it was too soon—that it would throw me back into my terrible depression, from which I'd just recently emerged.

When Candida came back to us a year later as planned, we had terrible fights. "But you can't wear that out! It's like a bathing suit!" she'd say nervously.

"Daddy said I could wear it," I'd counter. "LEAVE ME ALONE!"

She looked at me in silence as I, coquette that I was, admired myself in the mirror, ignoring her.

She'd give me warnings like, "It's minus five degrees today, don't forget your coat." And I'd turn on her, furious: "Do you still think I'm three years old!"

My father had bought and fixed up the concierge's apartment for her, but she only went downstairs to sleep. She must have been terribly lonely; Maria was now married, had two daughters who were Candida's godchildren and she did not have much time for her old friend.

Candida would walk into my room without knocking so often that I finally asked my father to put a lock on it, which he did. Then they must have made some kind of agreement. She stopped bothering me about my clothes and dates, and never said another word about missing the way it used to be between us.

* * *

Two years later, when I was fifteen, my father decided he'd had enough of France and sold our apartment. It was decided—by my father or Candida, or both—that she would not come along to America. With fabulous recommendations from my parents, she found a comfortable job as a housekeeper for an elegant, elderly French couple.

"Why don't you take care of babies, Didi?" I asked her.

"Ah *non*," she said, throwing up her hands. "*Jamais de la vie!*" Not on your life, said she.

Bewildered, frightened, looking forward to the future, I packed up my room. With Candida's help, it took me two full days. I kept only the most precious mementos.

My poor old Barbie dolls and teddy bears were brought out from the top storage space in the closet, dusty and gnarled and looking miserable. They all had handmade clothes, crocheted sweaters and slippers, flowery gowns and hats, made with care by Candida and her mother over the years.

"I'll clean them and give them to the poor," Candida said. "Don't you preoccupy yourself with them now, there's too much to do. Don't you preoccupy yourself."

In a drawer, we found the tiny wooden clogs Candida had brought me back from Portugal as a souvenir when I was six.

Cupping them in her hand, Candida said, "You know, I still have your first pair of shoes."

Our old Enrico Macias records were deep in the back of the closet, piled in a cardboard box. I had completely forgotten that I had been crazy about Enrico Macias. He was totally uncool now, the brunt of many jokes at school. Kids said contemptuously that only old ladies and fags went to the Olympia to see Enrico Macias.

He had been our entertainment on Saturday nights, long ago—we'd dance in my room to Enrico's crazy gypsy love songs; I'd stand on Candida's feet and she'd twirl me around from corner to corner, laughing and singing in a loud voice.

"I adore him," she'd say, red in the face, a hand over her heart.

Smiling up at us from the dusty jacket at the top of the pile was Enrico, fat-cheeked, curly-headed, happy as ever, impervious to the fickle nature of his fans' hearts.

"What do you say, Didi, shall we listen to a song?"

"Oh, no," she chuckled. "Not now. There's too much to do."

A sudden flood of emotion rose in my throat and I had to stare at Enrico's smiling face for a long while before I could talk.

"Here, you keep them, Didi." I handed her the box.

She took it from my hands and lovingly wiped the dust off Enrico's face with the flat of her hand.

"And here, keep the clogs too."

"You'll always be my little girl," she said, looking down at the little lacquered, hand-painted shoes.

A taxi came to take us to the airport. Candida stood in the street, in a black dress with a flowered scarf around her neck. She waved a white handkerchief, smiling bravely as we drove away. I watched her and waved frantically from the backseat. The taxi hadn't gone ten meters when her face collapsed, and marblelike tears began to tumble from her eyes.

NEW YEAR'S EVE

It snowed heavily on Christmas Day and my brother and I went out to build our first snowman in America. Our family had moved into an old colonial farmhouse on the eastern end of the South Fork of Long Island the previous spring. We had left Paris shortly after our father suffered his second attack of congestive heart failure. He had come home from the American Hospital of Paris fifteen pounds thinner and there was a look of resignation in his eyes which frightened us all.

"I always intended to go home when you kids got to be teenagers. You're already fifteen and I've waited longer than I intended to at first." No one spoke as he paused for a breath. He had gathered us around the antique oak table in the dining room, which was where most plans were proposed and discussed. My brother and I watched our mother's placid eyes for a clue but received none. Our father went on: "I want you kids to be real Americans. Anyway, I'm tired of Europe, the phones don't work. The plumbing's for shit. Nothing works properly. I want to go home."

Our family ran according to our father's own form of democracy; Billy and I and our mother could vote against him on any proclamation he made, but he held the right to veto the vote if all three of us voted against him. On that day, no one said a word in protest but our faces all wore crestfallen expressions. We understood instinctively from the sad and slightly guilty look on his face that he was not only talking about the phone system or the plumbing, he was talking about his heart, which he would not entrust to French doctors, even if they were hired by the American Hospital.

Our father went on to explain what was wrong with him. His heart had suffered scarring from the malaria he'd caught in the Pacific during the War. He told us that his friend had found us a house in the little resort town by the sea, that it would be a quiet place in winter, which was what he needed to continue to write the enormous book about the war that he had been working on for five years already.

By our first Christmas in America, our father's health had deteriorated so much that he could no longer leave the house because of the cold. Billy and I continued to behave as though he could still manhandle us, which, emotionally, he could. His strength of character had not deteriorated with the weakening of his body, which was now like a seventy-year-old man's. He spent most afternoons in a rocking chair between the fireplace and a large window in the living room, reading a book.

On that Christmas afternoon, as Billy and I rolled our snowman together, we witnessed an extraordinary sight: The young rosebuds on the split-rail fence at the bottom of the hill which had turned from pink to vermillion overnight in the first November frost, had not withered and fallen off the bushes. In the vast expanse of snow, they stood out like specks of fresh blood on a sheet. Billy and I abandoned our snowman and approached the fence. The roses seemed to be growing still in the complete desolation of white, stubbornly defying nature's onslaught. We ran up the hill toward the house, yelling.

We barged into the living room dragging in stacks of snow. Our father was sitting by the window looking out. He was dressed in one of the cotton nightshirts he had ordered especially from Brooks Brothers, and a warm blue robe and slippers. I was suddenly struck by the thinness and paleness of his ankles, by the fact that the veins were thick and the same color as the robe. Not wanting to shatter the mood my brother and I had rushed in with, I yelled out excitedly,

"DADDY! You wouldn't believe it! The roses are still growing on the fence. Come and see!"

I was out of breath and enveloped in a cloak of icy air
which had followed me into the room.

My father shuddered almost imperceptibly. Billy ran off
to shut the door.

"I'd love to, baby, but you know I can't. I can't even
make it up the goddamn stairs," he said evenly.

"Where's your camera, I'll take a picture," I offered, my
voice almost disappearing completely. I became paralyzed
when the severity of his illness struck me; like a house hit by
lightning, my entire system seemed to shut down.

"Good idea," he said, and smiled wanly.

When the pictures came back from Fotomat a few days
later, I spread them out on the same oak table that had once
inhabited our Paris dining room. Now it was in the long,
amber-colored kitchen. The pictures turned out marvelously
and I was ecstatic. "Look at this one!" I said, "and look at
this!" There was the dark brown fence, the dark brown rose
stems, the dark brown house in the background, and the
vermillion roses against the white, white snow and the
white, white sky. My father gazed at them for a long time
and then a solitary tear fell from his eye. He wiped it away
absently with the back of his hand.

"Daddy," I mumbled, "what's the matter?"

"They're beautiful," he said. "They make me feel sad."

Billy's and my first semester at the local high school had
been a miserable one. The local kids had not befriended us.
It seemed the locals were becoming slightly schizophrenic
due to the radical change the summers brought to the town.
They disliked and mistrusted but also adulated "New York-
ers," which included anyone who had not been born and
raised locally, like the corn and potatoes the area was
famous for.

Our schoolmates were the sons and daughters of the
firemen, the store owners, the fishermen, the farmers,
anyone who kept the town running for people like us who
were only supposed to invade in summer. Since September,
Billy had gained fifteen pounds and a thousand pimples on
his face and back and had taken to hibernating in front of

the television set. He would not talk to anyone, including our father, for days on end.

In September my father had persuaded me to join a local theater group and I became friendly with the actors and stagehands who were older and more sophisticated than the high-school kids. I fell madly in love but I would not tell anyone with whom.

One day my father made my mother and me sit down in the kitchen and he said in a neutral voice, "It's time to discuss sex."

"It's a little late for that," I said apprehensively.

"But don't you need birth control?" my mother said in a shaky voice. "My God, what have you been using up till now?"

"Rubbers," I said, and not another word.

"All right," my father said. "We'll call the doctor tomorrow. You don't have to tell us anything you don't want to tell us, but if you want to tell us, you can."

The reason I would not tell them was that the object of my passions was the twenty-nine-year-old carpenter who built the sets for the Playhouse. Dave had thin green eyes and a red beard. He had been in Vietnam but would not talk about it. I had already tried everything with him—all the things my father had warned me about continuously back in Paris—starting with alcohol and sex and working up to marijuana and cocaine, twice.

Dave had been married once, and had other women, including an older actress from the Playhouse. This woman, at least ten years my senior, despised me. I was no competition for her and stood frozen while she attacked my acting and called me an overprotected, spoiled brat during rehearsals. I could not help myself concerning the carpenter; I was obsessed with him and would not give him up. He often tried to warn me not to become attached to him. "I can't get involved with you. I'm still trying to figure out who I am," he would say.

At twenty-five I would never have looked at him. He would have seemed petty and cowardly and vain. But at that time, Dave filled some kind of void in my life which I was incapable of understanding. It seemed that he loved me when he took me for long drives in his station wagon and when he cooked hotdogs for me in his trailer. Then he would disappear for days. Dave would never call my house, and at first this seemed perfectly normal. But then I would call him for days on end, allowing the phone to ring up to twenty times, but he would not answer and would not show up at the Playhouse. I thought I might collapse from a short-circuit of emotions, because I loved and hated him so much at the same time. Promising myself never to speak to him again, I would go to rehearsal determined and end up in his trailer once again.

My father told me he was worried about me. I was becoming too thin and too quiet. After my lonely school days, he began to teach me to drive his Volkswagen on the winding back roads.

He never asked me about my lover. He would teach me about driving, about hitting the gas when I turned into a curve and about never panicking. Always expect the unexpected, he would say. And once in a while he would offer to listen if I wanted to talk to him or ask him questions. I would not talk.

He went four times to see the play I was in, *The Cat and the Canary,* in which I played a thirty-five-year-old neurotic old maid. My father sat in the first row and watched only me. He gave me sound advice.

"Don't ever look out at the audience," he told me. "The audience doesn't exist." I told him I wanted to be an actress when I grew up. He told me acting was the toughest job in the world and that actresses are treated "like shit." This made me want desperately to tell him about the carpenter, but I knew that if I did, my father would have pulled me out of the Playhouse and threatened Dave with one of his shotguns.

Driving with my father was the one thing besides seeing the carpenter that I looked forward to that fall. Then suddenly, during the last week of October, my father got sick again and the carpenter disappeared forever.

Billy and I came rushing home from school on an afternoon that was like any other afternoon in the late fall. The school bus dropped us off across the street and we ran up the driveway, over a red and gold crackling carpet of leaves, to find an ambulance parked by the back door. Our father was coming down the brick path on a stretcher. A brown wool blanket covered his body and was tucked in at his sides. Leaves swirled all around him like an escort of frantic, rust-colored birds. Our mother was walking beside the stretcher, holding his hand. Her face was pale and drawn. Billy and I stood watching, clutching our books by the ambulance's doors.

Our father gave us an apologetic look and raised the hand our mother was not holding. "No driving class today, honey," he said to me. "Billy, will you rake up these leaves when you get a chance? Don't worry, you two. You hear? I'll be home soon."

After trying to call Dave for four days, I found out from someone in the theater group that he had up and moved to Florida in his trailer, taking along the older actress who had gotten pregnant. I figured the woman had done it on purpose and I wished every misery in the world upon them. I was ashamed when the woman returned less than a year later without him and with a baby named Biscayne Bay.

I thought that all boys would understand sex the way Dave had. Something terrible and frantic was happening inside me and I had no idea what it meant. I was hungry all the time, but not for food—I stopped eating almost completely after my father went into the hospital—I wanted things, wanted to be loved, accepted, understood.

I did not correlate the high-school boys' sudden interest in me with the disappearance of Dave. Finally Janet, the girl who sat next to me in homeroom, told me: they all knew. Everyone in school knew that I had had an affair with an older man.

My father was in the hospital for three weeks, during which time I had sex with a basketball player, a surfer, a farmer's son, and a boy who worked in his father's auto body shop after school. After each urgent, hurried embrace in the scratchy backseat of some parent's car, parked in the dark corners of the woods and each cold, indifferent stare I was subjected to the next day I felt more lonely and more hungry and more frantic to find whatever it was I was looking for. I understood that they did not care a damn about me or how I felt or that my father was in the hospital, but I could not help myself when they turned all sweet with me and coaxed my clothes off in their dirty, chilly cars.

I could not discuss this with anybody and I worried constantly that someone would say something to my brother in school. But Billy never mentioned a word; he was dealing with his own worries. Every day after school he took the rake out from the barn and attacked the lawn. He raked with a passion he showed for nothing except the television. After the third day of this I watched our mother walk out of the kitchen into the yard, pulling a cardigan together over her chest. The wind made the screen door flutter on its hinges. "Billy, you don't have to do it every day! Wait till all the leaves fall!" she cried out in a desperate voice. Billy said nothing. The leaves kept falling, there was a new carpet of them each afternoon. They twirled about in that frantic way, falling all around as Billy kept raking until all the trees were bare and the lawn was bare and brown.

Our father came back a week before Thanksgiving. His face had always been strong-featured, not particularly angular but radically defined. Now he looked like an American Indian with his high, flat cheekbones jutting out above the dark caves of his cheeks. His large, square chin seemed larger than ever without any fat to fill out the upper part of his face. He looks great, I thought, strong as a bull. He could still scare anybody with that face, he could still beat the shit out of anybody.

It was a quiet time in the house. Our father was working ten-hour days, trying to finish the book he told us he was afraid he would not have time to finish. We told him he shouldn't talk like that; he was going to go on for another twenty years. Two elevator chairs were installed in the stairwells that led up to the third floor so that he could make it up to his office to write every day. No one but him seemed to take this as an ominous sign. When a thing degenerates slowly, people tend not to notice. Each little decline is only compared to the previous decline and not to the relative whole.

The long Thanksgiving weekend gave me too much time to think about the boys I'd had sex with who would no longer even say hello to me in the school's halls. This preoccupied me so much that I hardly thought about anything else.

On Sunday morning, after a sleep filled with nightmares, I climbed the stairs to my father's office and knocked lightly on the door. As always, he did not like to be disturbed while he was working but this seemed important enough to me to interrupt him: I was finally ready to ask him for advice.

My father was sitting in his leather office chair on wheels, glasses on and paper in the typewriter. The large, white room felt cold to me and the sweat on the back of my neck seemed to turn to ice.

"Daddy, I have to talk to you."

"What is it, baby?"

He did not look up from the sheet of paper stuck in the typewriter.

"I don't want to go back to school here, Daddy."

"What happened? What's the matter?"

"They hate me."

"They don't hate you," he said evenly. "They don't know what to make of you because you've come from somewhere else."

"I did some bad things, Daddy," I said in a desperate voice. "I feel so guilty. These guys, they're really nice before and stuff but then they won't talk to me anymore. And now I have to go back to school with them and I'm so scared."

He thought about this awhile, rubbing his temples and mussing up his thin curly hair.

"How was it, I mean, did you enjoy it?"

At the time this question seemed absurd to me; later on, in college, I thought about that day and believed that I understood what he'd been aiming at. In college I made friends with a girl who kept a notebook with a scoresheet on the boys she slept with, who told me that she never had reached orgasm with a man. Sex to her was as inconsequential and impersonal as shaking hands. I decided after talking to my friend that my father had probably been wondering if he'd been too free, if I'd misconstrued his liberal attitude toward sex.

I looked around at his office, at the papers shoved into precarious piles everywhere, at the photographs of the roses on the wall behind the typewriter, and said uncomfortably, "There was only one, you know. It was good with him. He was older."

"How much older?"

"Much older."

"*My* age?" I saw that my father was getting red around the ears, and I became frightened that his heart would act up again. My father angry was a terror to be reckoned with.

"No, younger."

"Who?"

"This guy from the Playhouse."

"Which one?"

"Dave. The guy who built the sets." I figured it was all right to tell him since Dave was now living in a trailer somewhere down in Florida.

"Goddamn it," my father said. "I sat with that guy more than once down at the pub. He's the one who was in 'Nam. No wonder he was looking at me with that shit-eating grin. He probably thinks I'm an idiot. Jesus Christ. I knew there was somebody but I thought it was one of the kids. If I'd known I would have threatened to throw his ass in jail." And after a moment he asked, "And it was all right with him, though, with Dave?"

"Yes. But he left." Now I started to cry; it was as though three months' worth of tears had finally built up enough pressure to collapse my internal dam.

My father patted the arm of his chair and I went around the desk to him. I sat on the floor by his skinny legs and put my head down on his lap. He ran his fingers through my hair as he had when I'd been little. The only difference was that now he could not take me on his lap.

"Sex is like tennis," he said.

"Like *tuh-tennis*?" I said, sobbing against his bony knees.

"Yes, just like tennis. You have to learn to play. You just

don't walk out on a court with a racket and play like Chris Evert. And of course, you can practice against a wall but that's not playing with somebody else. Boys your age don't know fuck-all about sex. You think you're doing them a favor by sleeping with them and that they'll be grateful to you, but not at all. They think you're bad afterward. And that's just ridiculous, but that's the way it is."

"You weren't like that, were you?"

"Sure I was. It took me years to figure it out."

"They're going to call me a slut in school now," I said dismally.

"Well, the hell with them," he said. He thought for a while and then added, "This move has been hard on you kids, I know. And since I've been sick I haven't been there for you much. This book is driving me crazy. I've got to finish it. Your brother sits in front of that goddamn TV like a glom and nothing I say will make him move his ass. What am I supposed to do? Lock him in his room? Throw a football with him? I can't even climb the stairs. He's at that awkward age. You passed it pretty quickly. With boys it takes longer. You've got to try to be nice to him."

"He won't talk to me."

"I know . . . The school's not a bad school, I suppose, as far as public schools go. I guess I've got to be there for you kids more. See, I'm selfish too. I don't care so much about dying, it's leaving my book that worries me."

His dying was the farthest thing from my mind. It was simply not a possibility. I had never heard him use that word before and fear, like two clawed hands, gripped at my stomach and throat.

"Don't say things like that, not even as a joke."

"I'm not joking. What am I supposed to do, lie to you? I'm sick. I don't know how long I can last."

"But they said twenty years."

"Or five years," he said simply. There was no fear in his voice, just the acceptance of a plain and simple fact. We listened to the humming of the heating pipes and the electric typewriter for a while.

"I'm so glad you came up to talk to me," he said. "I figured if you wanted to, you would. Backseats and drive-ins and beaches are no place to have sex, baby. Especially the beach. Ugh, I hate that sand. I'm glad I'm such an old man because if you'd been fifteen ten years ago, I might have blown a gasket over this. But now I understand things I didn't back then. There's so much I wish I could tell you but I don't know how. Listen, be smart about this now. They'll figure you're easy and keep on trying with you. Just say no till you find someone you really like. When you find someone you really like, come talk to me. All right?"

"All right."

"Listen, since I really can't take you driving anymore, how about let's start reading books together?"

"What kind of books?"

"Novels. So you'll be a little ahead of the game when you get to college. Not the short stories they give you to read in the high school, you know. Books *I* like."

He started me off with *A Farewell to Arms* which made me cry so much at the end that I stayed in bed for an entire day. Then we read *The Great Gatsby* and then *Light in August*. *Light in August* was by far the most difficult thing I'd ever tried to read in my life. We would sit in the living room by the crackling fireplace in the late afternoons. My father told me about the souls of books, how they came out of the writer whole, like babies with their own separate souls. "But with books," he told me, "once they're finished you don't have to worry about what's going to happen to them when you're gone."

Two weeks before Christmas vacation began, Keith Carter from my high-school drama class asked me if I needed a ride home after a rehearsal of *Animal Farm*. Keith was reading the part of Napoleon the pig. He had a deep voice and put *a*'s on the end of *er* words, and *er*'s on words that ended in *a*'s. His legs were thin as sticks but his back was shaped like a V from lifting weights. Janet, the girl from homeroom, told me that Keith had quit football after a fight with the coach and had been in trouble with the police for breaking and entering a friend's house on a lark. People in school respected him because the cops had tried to make a deal with him: You tell us who's the biggest dealer in the school and we won't press charges. Go to hell, Keith had said, and they pressed charges. He was only seventeen so they put him on probation. He lived in a shack "on the wrong side of the tracks" and his father was an alcoholic who'd gotten himself kicked out of the ambulance corps. Janet told me he'd "been around," slept with older women. I thought we had tons in common and was crazy about him long before he asked me if I needed a ride.

"I don't usually have the car," he said as he pulled up our driveway at ten-thirty that night. "I told my motha I'd do the lawn for her if she'd let me take it just one night. I been meaning to ask you if you needed a ride for weeks.

"Jesus," he said, and whistled as he peered out at the amber light that came from every window of the house from the ground floor to the attic, making it look like a Mississippi steamboat.

"I didn't know your folks were loaded."

"They're not that loaded," I said defensively. I thought for a second and then invited him in.

"Na," he said. "I'm not good with parents."

"Are you just giving a ride this one time or are you going to ask me out?"

"You wanna go out sometime?"

"You have to come in and ask my father."

"Jesus," he said. "I heard different about you." He got out and slammed the door.

My father was sitting in front of the TV in the kitchen. There was a serene expression on his face and he did not turn immediately as we came in. Keith changed suddenly, he stood up straighter, became almost respectful, and the expression of constant contempt he wore on his face disappeared. My daddy'll still scare the shit out of anybody, I thought proudly.

"Hi, Mr. Willis. Keith Carta," Keith said, putting out his hand. We sat down at the table on both sides of my father.

A car chase was proceeding, raising dust on the screen.

"I saw this movie," Keith said.

"It's kind of fun," my father said. "What's it called— *Thunderbolt and Motherfuck*—something like that."

113

Keith almost fell out of the chair. He leaned back and let out a howl of laughter that shook his whole body.

"Watch the chair," my father said. "It's Louis Treize."

"Louie who?" Keith said, still laughing. "Sorry." He righted himself.

My father asked him what he did with his free time. Keith told him he'd quit football after a fight with the coach and that now he was working for the highway commission after school.

"What was the fight about?" my father asked.

"Smoking cigarettes," Keith said evenly. "I told him he couldn't run my life."

"I used to be that way too," my father said, and chuckled.

"I want to save so I can buy a car," Keith said. "These people down the street, they have a sixty-three Mercedes that they want three hundred dollars for. It needs a new transmission, but it's still a steal." After a moment, he added simply, "I wanna take Channe out sometime."

"How're you going to take her out without a car?" my father asked.

"Borrow my motha's."

"Are you a good driver?"

"A very good driva. I figure you got to drive defensive, like in football. Everyone else is a danger coming straight at ya. I'll tell ya, Mr. Willis, the nuns are the worst drivers I ever saw."

My father was nodding slowly. "Can't drink and drive," he said.

"Neva."

"Well, if your mother won't let you have hers, you can take mine out once. Channe's got to be home by twelve."

"That's real nice of you, Mr. Willis. Real nice. Don't worry, I swea I'll drive careful and get her home by twelve."

Keith borrowed his older brother's girlfriend's ID and took me to Tides, a bar out in the middle of the woods. Three of the boys I'd had sex with were there playing pool. They said hello to Keith with straight faces and then actually said hello to me as though I were just another one of the local girls. I drank White Russians, a dozen of them, which were bought for me by the three boys and by Keith. I bought several rounds for them as well, with the twenty dollars my father had given me. I threw up out the window of Keith's mother's car. He was driving like Mario Andretti to get me home by twelve. We walked into the kitchen at 12:05. Keith was sweating. My father was sitting in front of the TV looking at his watch.

"Sorry, Mr. Willis. She kinda had too many drinks and got a little sick."

"Well, you shouldn't keep *buying* them for her," my father said, his thin mouth contorting into something between a snarl and a smile.

"I didn't. Some otha guys were. I tried to tell her to cool it but she wouldn't listen. She's stubborn."

"Next time, Channe, don't drink so much or I'm grounding your ass," my father said.

Keith and I made love in the back of his mother's station wagon on our second date. It was uncomfortable and cold even though Keith had brought blankets and had the heat up as high as it would go.

"I wish we didn't have to do this like this, Channe," he said against my neck.

"I know," I said.

"What kind of weird name is that, Channe? I can't get used to it. I mean, why can't you have a name like Betty?"

"It's Charlotte-Anne. My father's sister's name. She died before I was born."

"You rich people always have weird names."

He came in and said good night to my father, who gazed at us with a silly grin and then shook his head.

"Well, good night," Keith said. "I'll call you tomorrow."

"Where'd you go?" my father asked after Keith had left.

"Nowhere, just driving around."

"Sounds like fun," my father said.

I went to bed thinking I would never talk to Keith again. The phone rang at nine o'clock the next morning, which was a Sunday. It was Keith calling to ask if I wanted to go ice skating on the town pond.

Later, Keith's mother dropped us off at my house and Keith stayed for dinner. After dinner we all watched a movie on TV and then Billy went off to bed, grumbling "good night" without looking at anyone.

After the news, Keith got up to go.

"How're you getting home?" my father asked.

"Hitching," Keith said.

"It's so cold out," my father said. "Are you guys sleeping together yet?" he asked, as though it were just a continuation of the last sentence.

"Well—" Keith started, and I said, "Yes, Daddy."

"I don't want you kids doing it in cars. Especially not my car."

Keith laughed softly.

"I'd rather know where you are. I'd rather have you sleeping together under my own roof. So, I'll tell you what. Call your mother and tell her you're sleeping over and you can take the bus to school with Channe and Billy in the morning."

"Bill," my mother said as Keith went to the kitchen to call his mother, "isn't it a little soon? I mean, for God's sake—"

"I don't give a shit," he said simply. "They're going to do it anyway, let them do it right."

It was only another week before Keith moved in permanently. One more mouth to feed meant nothing to my father, whereas having one less to feed meant a great deal to Mrs. Carter. Mrs. Carter's kind, hard-set, patient expression did not waver when Keith and I would stop by after school to say hello. She did not complain or ask her son any questions.

In return for room and board, Keith began to do odd jobs for my father around the house. He knew how to fix things. He knew about plumbing and electricity and was a good painter. During Christmas vacation it also became Keith's responsibility to pick Billy up at the high school after his tutoring session in English.

One day Keith and I found Billy sitting alone on the

front steps of the school with a swollen, bloody lip. He was pale and his eyes sagged ashamedly. He seemed to have been crying. He walked toward the car without looking at us.

"What happened to you, Billy?" Keith said. Billy got in the back of the Volkswagen without saying a word.

"Steve Bates pulled my jacket over my head and punched me in the mouth. I had my back to him, I was looking inside my locker. I would've fought back but I was worried about my teeth." He started to cry after that. "My teeth, you know. Dad always says protect your teeth."

I felt a rage so fierce and helpless I could not even think of a thing to say. I did not know Bates or why he would have picked on my brother but I wanted to kill him.

"Fuckin' Master Bates. What a scumbag," Keith said. "I bet he wasn't alone either. That kid's the biggest chicken shit in the world. Wants to be six-five and is only five-eight. Hates the world for it. I'm going to kill him."

"No, don't," Billy said. "He'll just come after me again. Forget it."

"That dipshit'll be pumping gas for the rest of his life, never'll get out of this town. And you'll be a congressman or a lawyer or something and he'll be filling your car, sayin 'anything else, *Sir*?'. That's why he hates you, even if he doesn't know it. His father's an asshole drunk like my father and you guys have the best father in the world."

"Please don't tell Daddy," Billy said. "He'll get upset. Tell him I fell down."

After the Christmas snowfall, the temperature dropped and the roads iced over completely. My father did not want us to go out on New Year's Eve. "Too many drunks," he said. "And the roads are frozen solid. It doesn't matter how carefully *you* drive if some jackass comes speeding down the road at you in the wrong lane."

"Oh please, Daddy. There's this huge party down at Tides. Keith won't drink, I swear. I'll call you from the bar when we get there." At that moment, to go to Tides for the party seemed the most important thing in my life. To finally fit in, to be Keith's girlfriend in front of everybody. To get to talk to the girls who had ignored me; it was a night when everyone would be out and everyone would be happy.

"God do I hate to be a party poop," he said. "Let me think about it." Billy did not want to go out with Keith and me and my father did not want him to be home by himself, with his parents, on New Year's Eve. Billy said he'd rather be alone anyway.

At dinner, my father asked Keith, "You know what to do if you lose control on ice?"

"Yeah," Keith said. "You have to turn into the spin. Like, if the back end is swerving to the left, you turn the wheel to the left."

"That's right."

My mother's face looked drawn and there was a strange anger in her eyes. Her own father had died of a heart attack on New Year's Eve when she was sixteen, while she'd been at a dance.

"I hate New Year's Eve," she said in a subdued voice. "And I really think you should stay home with your father tonight."

"But it's such a special night!" I said.

"All right," my father said. "You can take the car. But I want you kids home by one-thirty."

"Daddy!"

"All right, two, then. Call me when you get to Tides."

Keith's face went red with pride.

"You bet," Keith said.

Keith put on a shirt and tie and jacket. I wore one of my mother's silk shirts and a long woolen skirt and high-heeled boots.

I went up to my parents' room to show my mother how I looked. I was all smiles and my heart was beating fast.

My mother was sitting alone, leaning on her knees, at the edge of the bed. A drink was dangling from her hand. She seemed to be listening to the wind which seeped through the cracks in the windows, making a sound like twenty harmonicas all playing a different tune. We could hear the television droning on in the kitchen below us.

"This could be his last one, you know," my mother said. It was the first time she had said anything ominous about my father's condition.

"How can you say that?" I said angrily.

"You're so selfish you can't see anything but yourself. It doesn't matter if you stay home or not," she said, pushing it all away from herself with a tired hand. "Go go go. Go have a good time."

Keith and I left them sitting in the kitchen in front of the TV. They were watching the crowds in Times Square. A cloud of steam hung over the crowd's collective breath.

"God am I glad I'm not there," my mother said.

The roads were so dark the trees seemed white in the headlights. The road through the woods wound dangerously and there were no other cars in sight.

Keith was in an ebullient mood.

"I can't believe he let us have the car!" he shouted, laughing. "Damn, your old man is great. Maybe next year he'll be all right and we can all go out together. Dancing or something. Wouldn't that be great?"

Next year. Would we have anything to celebrate on New Year's Eve? I wondered. I saw my family sitting quietly, resignedly, in front of the TV set and my heart constricted in my throat.

"He's never going to be all right," I said, choked by tears.

"What are you talking about?"

"With what he's got you don't get better. You stay the same or you get worse. Turn back, Keith."

"WHAT?"

"Turn back, please. I want to be with them."

"Come on, Channe. The guys are waiting for us. The band's going to be great. It's New Year's Eve already. We'll get to dance together like you always say you want to do."

We headed on through the icy night. Keith squeezed my knee and talked about happy things, about how lucky I was to have a father like that, but I couldn't shake the feeling that we should have turned back.

Tides was packed with people. I waited for the phone by the bar for a long time. My turn came as people were getting ready to shout the countdown. The phone rang three times before my father picked up.

"Daddy," I said, barely able to control the shaking in my voice. BINGO! Midnight, everybody was screaming and kissing behind me.

"Happy New Year, Daddy," I said.

"Happy New Year, baby," he said.

"I wish I was home with you."

"It's quiet here," he said. "Your brother and I are having a tiny drop of champagne and your mother's finishing the bottle." He laughed quietly into the phone.

"Daddy. I wish I'd stayed home."

"It's all right, baby," he said in a soothing voice. "Have a great time for all of us."

The shouting around me was so intense I could barely hear him. I blocked one ear with my hand and listened to my father tell me that everything in my life was going to turn out just fine.

"Just as long as you don't marry Keith," he said. "It's fine to have an affair and all but I'm scared to death he's going to ask you to marry him and that you'll give up your whole future."

"Don't you worry, Daddy. I'm going to go to college."

"I love you," he said. "See you tomorrow."

I stepped outside without my coat, into the parking lot that was filled with cars. The air was bitterly cold. I looked up at the stars which swam in and out of focus like a million fireflies above my head. Without my father, the world meant nothing, and I had abandoned him on New Year's Eve.

"Please, God," I thought. "Please, if you exist. Please make it be all right."

There was a fence at the end of the parking lot but the rosebushes on it were dead. They looked like weeds, barren and black against the snow.

"Please, one more winter," I said, tears falling from my eyes. "Even if it means a wheelchair."

Keith was suddenly behind me, he placed my coat over

my shoulders and hugged me. He wrapped his arms tightly around me from the back.

"Let's go," he said. "If we hurry we can make it back in fifteen minutes. We can still have a glass of champagne with him."

CITIZENSHIP

My brother Billy and I are now twenty-seven. He recently called me at my office in the private school where I teach French, to tell me that his naturalization papers had finally come through. He was calling from his bank, which he usually does when he has something personal or important to say to me. It is his armor—to be in his stuffy business mode and unable, due to the surroundings, to get emotionally involved.

He asked offhandedly if I would accompany him the next Wednesday morning to the courthouse in Brooklyn. I was so pleased I jumped out of my chair, shouting, "YES! Of course!" into the phone.

His papers had been so long in clearing that waiting for his citizenship had become an obsession with him. The government took his French passport away three-and-a-half years ago, and since then he'd been, as he termed it, "A man without a country." He had no identity papers and was not permitted to travel abroad.

It was because his adoption by our American parents, first in France in 1965 and then at home a few years later, had been completely illegal—the result of many bribes and many contacts in high-up places.

"Are you asking Mom to come, too?" I asked, trying to sound nonchalant.

"No," he said vaguely. "It takes about four hours and she'd be bored to death."

He is mad at our mom—she has a new beau, the first one since our father died. The beau is a jackass of the highest order but we kept our mouths shut in the beginning. All our family friends said, "Give him a chance; he's good for her; she needs a man." Then a couple of months earlier, the beau moved into our house on Long Island. Within two weeks he'd taken down seventy-five percent of the photographs of our father and replaced them with ones of himself at a Hampton lawn party, dressed in his Australian outback attire and flanked by his two pet emus on leashes. In the photos, he is holding his hunter's hat (complete with crocodile-skin hatband) against his chest, and he and the emus are wearing a haughty expression. Their eyes are crinkled up as though against a harsh desert sun, and their small heads are stretched high on thin necks. A few strands of hair on the beau's balding head flutter about like the emus' downy black feathers. They look so much like a family that the pictures are quite frightening.

My brother and I have always gone home for most weekends, especially in summer. The recent change in the photographic decor caused quite a stir with us. In a rare display of emotion, Billy yelled at our mom. He told her that he'd never met such an arrogant, vain, foolish, childish son of a bitch in his life as this new beau.

"He's eccentric!" our mom cried out defensively; "I have a right to go on with my life!"

I wouldn't have said anything but the beau had taken to badgering us in front of dinner guests. There wasn't a thing in the world Billy and I could do that he couldn't do better. ("You were Phi Beta Kappa the second semester of your senior year? Well, *I* was Phi Beta the first semester of my junior year. The only one, too . . .") So I put in my two cents. "He's no eccentric, he's a poseur. Face it, Mom. He's so vain he's varicose."

After that, we stopped going home on weekends even though it was mid-August and unbearably hot in the city. Our mother took to calling us Electra and Hamlet over the phone, which made my blood curdle and the beau roar with laughter in the background.

Our mother was mortified when she learned that Billy

hadn't invited her to his naturalization. She told me the beau told her that's what she got for raising two spoiled rotten, ungrateful brats.

I admit I vacillated between feeling an evil pleasure and a terrible aching guilt over Billy's cold-heartedness. I did not want to interfere but finally, a few days before the big event, I called Billy at work and tried to get him to capitulate.

"Listen," I said in a complacent, matter-of-fact tone, "tell her she can come if she wants but she has to leave the beau at home."

There was a silence on the other end of the line.

"No," Billy said flatly.

I'd thought I might convince him to stop being angry at our mother just long enough to allow her to come to the ceremony, but no. I should have known better; he'd been stubborn since the day he'd entered our lives over twenty-two years before.

* * *

As a child, the two aspects of our background that thrilled my brother the most were that our maternal grandfather Antonio Cappuccino had been a rather notorious gangster, and that our father had fought in World War II.

"Did you kill lots of Germans, papa?" he asked one day, approaching our father gingerly. Our dad was sitting alone at the head of the long dining room table, having a hamburger for lunch. He took a break in his writing between one and two and on the days we were home, we descended on him with a million obscure questions.

"I killed some Japanese," our father said mildly. "But I never made it to Europe because I was wounded in the Pacific." One thing about our dad was that you were certain to get a straightforward answer to your question, no matter how painful the Truth might be. This was scary, but consistent.

"Someone *shooted* you?" Billy asked, wide-eyed and enthusiastic.

"Shot. No, it was shrapnel from a bomb. I was wounded twice. Once in the head and once in the leg."

My brother's face sagged in disappointment.

"Killing is no fun," our dad continued in that even tone. "It's horrible. Once I had to stab a man with my knife. Poor

Jap bastard was half starved to death but he was coming straight at me screaming with his bayonet out. I took his wallet, you see." He put his palms together then unfolded his hands like a book. "There was a photograph of a young woman with a baby in her arms." He pointed to his left palm. "I couldn't read what she wrote on the back. It was in Japanese . . . Crazy bastard." Tears fell from his olive-green eyes while his face remained hard-set and expressionless. He pushed the tears away indifferently while my brother stared at him, perplexed and slightly embarrassed.

"I swore I'd never kill anyone ever again. I think the only way I could ever kill someone was if a person tried to hurt you kids or your mother." He said this in a neutral tone, his green eyes glaring with intent, which made his words even more emphatic. There wasn't a doubt in my mind that he would do just that. "And that's about the only reason I'd kill anyone anymore." His voice trailed off.

My brother had a general aversion to displays of emotion. He turned pale and lowered his eyes whenever a person shouted or cried or pleaded. The only times I ever saw him show emotion were when we watched slapstick comedies, Charlie Chaplin or Laurel and Hardy. He'd sit wide-eyed and licking his lips in front of the television, bracing himself for the next gut-wrenching laugh. He'd turn red as a beet and laugh so hard, kicking up his feet, that he'd fall backwards out of his chair. Watching him was more amusing than watching the movies, which I found idiotic, and made certain to tell him so at every opportunity. "I can't be*lieve* you like those idiots!" I'd hiss, and he'd gaze at me with the droopy-eyed look of a dog who knows he's done something wrong and has now just to endure the punishment to be once again left alone. Oh, how I had hated that look.

Our first month in kindergarten at the École de Lorraine did not go well for Billy. My parents had asked me to "look out for him," but I was embarrassed by him. From the very first day, our teacher singled him out to ridicule, to use as the brunt of all her jokes.

Our teacher was never able to break him, and came to

hate that doggish look of his even more than I did. One day he scribbled all over his notebooks; big, dark knots of color from corner to corner. The teacher grabbed him by the ear, dragged him to the outer hallway and shoved him into the hanging coats. She slammed the door on him and turned toward us, wiping her hands against each other as though to say it was a job well done.

The scene caused in me the most agonizingly ambivalent feelings. I hated the woman, wanted to attack her, bite her legs, cry out, "It's not fair!" But I also felt so safe and invisible in my neutrality that I loved her for not despising *me*. I never said a word.

From that day on, Billy spent a good deal of time out in the hall with his face in the coats.

After about a month, my mother took me aside one afternoon and asked me apprehensively, "So, how's Billy doing in school?"

"I don't know," I responded, shrugging. "Mademoiselle Fournier always puts him in the *vestiaire*."

"*Vestiaire*? What the hell is that?" Her dark-blue eyes went round and the corners of her mouth began to twitch.

"The coat closet, you know."

"Whatever for?" my mother cried out.

"She doesn't like him more than she doesn't like anybody else."

I followed my mother down to Billy's room. He was hunched over his new Civil War fort and hand-painted, Confederate and Union lead soldiers that our dad had ordered all the way from F.A.O. Schwarz in New York City. Our father held a special admiration for Robert E. Lee and his troops (although he was quick to point out that he was on the side of the Union) and had apparently passed these feelings on to Billy. My brother had lined up all the blue soldiers on one side of the fort, and the grays on the other, and seemed to be having trouble deciding who would have the fort for today's battle.

"Billy, why didn't you tell me that Mademoiselle Fournier puts you in the *vestiaire*?"

"I don't know," my brother said, looking at his soldiers.

No matter how much our mom cajoled, he wouldn't say another word.

The next afternoon she came to fetch us at school. We were in the courtyard, standing in line on the dusty gravel, waiting with the rest of our class for our mothers and nannies. We were surprised to see our mother because Candida usually came to get us.

She marched up to Mademoiselle Fournier, who was of indeterminate age and had dark hair like steel wool, and said in her almost incomprehensible French, "So, Madam, why is my son always in the *vestiaire?*"

"*Pardon?*" said Mademoiselle Fournier with a contemptuous expression.

"Oh, come on, you understand me perfectly well," said our mom. "Channe, translate for me, will you?"

"*Ma mère voudrait savoir,*" I said, looking up at Mademoiselle, "*pourquoi mon frère est toujours dans le vestiaire.*"

Mademoiselle turned to our mother with a haughty air and said, "Well, today it was because he threw sand in a boy's eyes."

"Sand?" asked my mother. "Sand? What do you mean?"

"*Oui, du sable, parfaitement!*" She pointed toward the gravelly, sandy ground of the courtyard. Our mom bent over and picked up a handful of dirt in her gloved fist and threw it into Mademoiselle's face.

"Well, here's some sand for you, you *bitch!*" she shouted in English. All the mothers and children turned toward us. Mademoiselle cried out and brought her hands to her eyes, our mom grabbed us by the wrists and dragged us, running as fast as she could, through the large double doors of the school's main entrance.

The next day we were registered at the École Bilingue Internationale.

An amazing trait of my brother's was that, although I was unwilling to stick up for him in difficult situations, he showed an almost fanatical loyalty to me.

In the fall of our seventh year, a boy at Bilingue named Didier yanked my gray pleated uniform skirt up to my chest during recreation, while several other boys stood around and jeered.

God knows, I was such a flirt I probably deserved it. Didier was one of the boys I couldn't stay away from. I was infatuated with boys who had an unruly look to them, and Didier was the unruliest of the lot. No matter how often a teacher told him to tuck his shirt in, his shirttails hung out of his shorts in back. He always had a new bruise or cut, one gray sock invariably had lost its elastic and sagged in folds around his ankle, and his shock of brown hair stood out at all angles from his head. The day before, I had allowed him to kiss me behind a stone statue, and today he had yanked up my skirt. What injustice!

My brother approached me with a certain amount of discomfort as I sat off to the side, crying and humiliated, on a stone park bench. We were in the same grade but a different class, and shared the same recreation spot—it was a long, pebbled alley lined with trees in the Champs de Mars Park below the Eiffel Tower. Stuttering, I reported what had happened while he frowned over me.

"Which one?" he asked looking toward the group of boys in the distance. They had resumed their game and were running around in wild circles, laughing, having already thoroughly forgotten the incident.

I pointed out Didier, who was almost a head taller than the others. He was big for a French boy.

My brother gazed at the pack for a long moment, thinking. Finally, he said, "Well, I guess I'm going to have to go say a thing to him."

Billy sighed, shoved his hands into the front pockets of his shorts, and set off toward the pack. Seriously worried, I followed a few steps behind. It was clear Billy had made up his mind and trying to talk him out of it wasn't going to do any good.

He walked right into the middle of the pack and tapped Didier on the shoulder. It was reassuring that they were approximately the same size. Billy said, *"Je m'appelle Billy Willis et tu viens d'attaquer ma soeur"*—My name is Billy Willis and you just attacked my sister.

Didier spun around, the game stopped, and silence fell around them. I kept a few feet behind Billy.

"If you say you're sorry I won't have to knock you down," Billy went on in the calmest of tones.

"Why should I?" said Didier, throwing him a suspicious glare and looking around for support. None of the other boys seemed to want to get involved (they were not as big as Didier or Billy) and to my profound relief they took a collective step backward.

"I'm going to count to three," Billy said. Didier put his hands on his hips and tapped his foot impatiently.

"*Un, deux, trois,*" Billy said. Then he pulled some kind of judo maneuver which involved kicking Didier's feet out from under him, and Didier fell to the ground.

"Sorry," Billy said, offering his hand to help Didier to his feet. Didier ignored him.

"It's just that I can't allow anyone to attack my sister."

Didier wiped the dirt off the back of his shorts.

"We're going to drop this for now," he said, and turned away. Under the circumstances, it probably seemed the reasonable thing to do.

"How did you learn to do that?" I mumbled as my brother and I walked off.

Blushing, he explained that there was a judo class on TV at eight A.M. on Saturdays. "I didn't really want to do that. He seemed like an all right boy."

"Whose side're you on anyway?" I said, punching him lightly in the arm.

That was one of the problems between us: It was not that he adored me so much that he was convinced I could do no wrong—it was the principle of the thing. I had been terrorizing him for three years now, with the help of Candida, who smacked him hard on the side of the head whenever a fight erupted between us.

Our father had forbidden him to hit me, and Billy never did, although he'd figured out numerous ways to wrestle me and pin me down without hurting me. His face bore the scars from my bites and scratches. I wasn't allowed to scratch or bite him, either, of course, but that didn't stop me.

Sometimes, if he was angry enough, he would pin me down, sit on my face, and fart. Sometimes I managed to bite his behind, but usually he was too quick. This drove me to madness.

If we were caught by our mother, red-handed in the middle of a fight, she automatically took his side, compensating, I gather, for Candida's bias toward me. Our mother was generally correct in her assumption, but the times that I was innocent and he was guilty but I was punished are the ones I remember. I was convinced she loved him better, and hated myself for not being able to get her to love me more.

If our mother ever asked him what was that new scratch on his face, he'd respond that he'd been playing with one of the Siamese cats. His unwillingness to report me must have come from his year in the children's home, where it probably was the little ones against the big ones, and no one with dignity tattled.

It hurt my feelings nevertheless that he felt he *had* to defend my honor simply because I was his sister, not because he adored me. But I admired him just the same.

That spring we were seven, the school gave our grade some form of French aptitude test and found that Billy could neither read nor write. Madame Beauvier, the *directrice*, called our father at home and he flew over to the school in a rage. I was in a class upstairs and we could hear his shouting echoing through the halls.

"What kind of school are you that you let a kid go three whole years before you realize he can't read: AND TAKE THAT SANCTIMONIOUS LOOK OFF YOUR FACE, IT MAKES ME WANT TO CHUCK YOU RIGHT OUT THE WINDOW!"

In the back of the car that afternoon, regaling in the fact that there was yet another thing I was better at than Billy, I asked him deliciously if it was true that he couldn't read or write.

He shrugged as though he were bored to death by everything and gazed out the window with an impassive expression.

It was only a few weeks before summer vacation and

Billy stayed in school until then. He was left alone, shunned by everyone, teachers and students alike.

An American girl called Susan who was so sugar sweet she made you want to throw up—a tall lean creature with large black eyes who was the boys' favorite because she knew the words to songs and knew a million different games she'd learned in the Girl Scouts—came up to me in the hallway between classes and said, "I'm really sorry to hear your brother's retarded." Her voice warbled so tragically you'd have thought somebody had died. She seemed to be enjoying this moment tremendously, as much as I'd enjoyed mine in the car. For a second I hated us both equally.

I responded, "What do you know about anything, you're a stupid cunt." I had no idea what this word meant, but knew it was just about the worst thing you could say because when my father said it, my mother yelled at him. "Goddamnit, Bill," she'd say, "don't talk like that in front of the kids. You're going to get us in trouble with those tight-ass parents of those embassy kids they go to school with."

Susan obviously did not know what the word meant either, because her face registered confusion, and then her condescending look became tinged with doubt. She was probably worried that I knew something she did not (which was in all honesty a rare occasion) and she let it go at that. But the next day, Susan's mother called the school and complained. The headmistress called me in and kindly asked me to refrain from such vulgarities, but she did not call my father; after the fiasco with my brother she doubtless wanted to avoid another confrontation with him.

We went to America for the summer, and my parents took Billy to one of the most famous and expensive psychiatrists in New York. Many years later, in a bar on Long Island, my brother told me his version of the story. It was at a time shortly after our father's death when we were particularly close, and he would ask me to go barhopping with him as a pretext to drink enough so that he could relax and tell me about things he otherwise would not. Billy confided that not learning to read French had been a conscious decision on his part; he'd wanted to be as American as possible and had decided that English would be the only language he would learn to read and write. They didn't offer English as a course, however, until third grade at École Bilingue Internationale.

My parents weren't big on psychiatry to start with, but they saw no other recourse since Billy refused to discuss his "problem" with them, although they'd approached the matter in a most unhysterical way:

"Billy," my mother said, "what's this crap you're learning disabled? You're the smartest kid I know. What's the problem?"

He looked up at her with those heavy, bored eyes, and shrugged.

In New York, my brother was given tests for the learning disabled while my mother discussed our family history privately with the psychiatrist. She was frank and candid, and told the doctor that my father was a writer with a busy social calendar and she, as his wife, wasn't home much and relegated most of the maternal duties to Candida, our Portuguese nanny. She told him they made sure to have dinner with us at least twice a week and that every Sunday, we had a family outing.

Billy had noticed in the psychiatrist's waiting room that our mother was quite anxious—when she was in this condition her mouth twitched at the corners. He became even more convinced (although our parents had told him over and over that it was simply a test to see why he couldn't learn to read) that the Americans were trying to decide whether our parents were fit to keep him. He'd had a few weeks to study up on what he thought the American Family was supposed to look like: he'd been religiously watching *The Brady Bunch* and *Leave It to Beaver* and several other sitcoms on the television in our hotel room.

"I think we're more like the *Addams Family*," he'd told me after a long and gloomy deliberation.

The psychiatric tests divulged that Billy was not learning disabled, and now it was time for his interview.

"It's very important that you tell me the truth," the psychiatrist said to Billy. Billy nodded vigorously.

"How are things at home?" the doctor asked.

"Very good," Billy said. "Mommy gets up every morning and makes breakfast and then she cleans, and then she does the laundry, and then she shines the shoes, and then she goes shopping, and then she makes *gouter* at four and dinner at seven-thirty."

The psychiatrist was perplexed.

"Is she a good cook?"

Billy gave this question some thought.

"No."

"Tell me about your daddy."

"He killed a man once with his bayonet and he said he'll do it again to anyone who tries to take me away from him," Billy said flatly.

"Nobody wants to do that," the doctor gently said. Billy glared at him, not remotely convinced.

"How do you like your school? Do you like your classmates and your teachers?"

"They're Frogs, mostly," he said, feeling patriotic. "I'd rather live in America."

"Why?"

"They have better TV here. And much better candy. And anyway we're American."

After their conversation, the doctor recommended that our mother spend more time with us at home, and diagnosed that my brother was having an identity crisis over his nationality. He felt the best cure would be to enroll Billy in a strictly American school. My parents wrote letters immediately.

By the end of the summer, Billy had been accepted to a private American school in Paris, entirely through the mail.

Our father took it upon himself to explain to us why we were living in France.

"You see," he said, "your mother won't live anywhere in America but New York City, and I can't write in New York. There's too much going on and it's too much fun." He watched us for a reaction and we stared back, perplexed. "We'll go on home when you kids get to be teenagers. Find someplace in between New York and peace and quiet. If we stay in France too long you'll grow up to be Eurotrash brats, like all our friends' kids did. They don't know who the hell they are."

We went home on the *SS France* at the end of the summer. Our mother told us she might be pregnant. "It's incredible," she said. "The doctor said I had a one-in-a-thousand chance of ever getting pregnant again. Well, it's been two and a half months. How do you kids feel about having a little brother or sister?" She seemed flushed, almost overwhelmed by her good fortune.

I was horrified. First they bring me this donkey of a kid who isn't even fun to play with and now there's going to be another one? I thought. And what if Candida loves the new baby more than me? Candida had gone to Portugal for the summer, to visit her mother. She sent us postcards in her unreadable, bastardized French that said things like, "Ay Channe my *bébé* I miss you so I can't wait for to see you back home. I kiss eberybody much."

On the *SS France*, our dad always paid for two tiny rooms in the bowels of Tourist Class, and then, because he was a well-known writer and knew how to tip and bribe without offending, the steward (for a certain fee) would move us to two free rooms on the Veranda Deck. The steward's tip was considerably less than the rooms would have cost our dad by going through normal channels, but that was not why he did it, he said. He just got a big kick out of screwing the System.

The Veranda deck was as chic as you could get and still be in Second Class—our parents didn't like First Class; they found it too stuffy and dull. My mother, however, got a special passkey to the First Class swimming pool, sauna, and massage center.

In the swimming pool of Second Class, an outdoor thing on an upper deck of the ship, Billy took to playing with the smaller children. The rocking of the ship made the water swish in big waves from side to side, and Billy swam around herding the littler children toward the middle to keep them from banging into the edges. He explained to them about the waves and stood in the shallow end and caught them as they jumped into the water, squealing with laughter. He even taught one little boy to swim without his floater. "You see," he explained gently, arms wrapped around the little waist, "your body is full of air too, just like a *bouée.*"

"What are you doing playing with little kids, Billy?" I asked him rather contemptuously.

Frowning, he responded, "I'm learning how to be a big brother. I've never been a big brother, so I'm learning." This seemed like the most obvious thing in the world to him. I started imagining that he and the new little brother or sister were going to gang up on me and make my life more miserable than it already was.

Our mother miscarried in the third month and Billy was inordinately gloomy for several weeks.

Our rooms were separated by an archway and one night I woke up to his sobbing in his bed. I went to him and sat down beside him. In the beginning these crying fits in the middle of the night had been frequent, but lately they had completely disappeared.

"What is it?"

"The baby went away because I'm here and there isn't enough room for him too."

"No, no, no! That's not it at all! There's lots of room! Mommy's sick, that's all."

It was like anything else I said to try to make him change his mind—useless. I shook him hard by the shoulder.

"Stop it! Stop it, do you hear me? IT'S NOT BECAUSE OF YOU!"

"Then maybe it's because of you. Because you're so terrible he didn't want to come live in our family."

It was almost as if he'd punched me right in the heart with all his strength.

Billy's American school, which our dad said cost as much a year as a brand-new car, did not have a cafeteria. Candida had to make Billy sandwiches every morning. She'd cut a fourth off a baguette and slice it down the middle. He'd get ham and butter or scrambled eggs and butter. Candida did not have much of an imagination when it came to sandwiches. After about a month, my parents received a letter from Billy's school:

Dear Mr. and Mrs. Willis:

We were not aware that your son is a scholar-ship student, attending our school under the aus-pices of the American Embassy or an overseas company. Apparently Billy has been sitting quietly through lunch break without having a thing to eat, and refuses the half a sandwich his little neighbor, Davey Smith, has been offering him. May I be so bold as to recommend our Lunch Program For the Needy? Many of our students whose parents are not able to afford to give their children a lunch box, take advantage of this program which will offer your child a well-balanced lunch, as well as one One-A-Day vitamin, daily, at no extra cost to you.

Sincerely,

Mrs. Harriet Mackenzie, Director
Lunch Program For the Needy

Our parents were stupefied.

Our dad was furious because, having been raised poor, he could not stand the waste of food. Our mom was beside herself because some of those "tight-assed Embassy peo-ple" were going to be under the impression we were destitute. And according to our dad, we were always almost destitute, until he finished another book. It seemed he'd celebrate finishing a book for a day, and the next day he was right back to worrying about starting the new one and keeping us from destitution. We worried when my father worried; but looking back, I believe none of us ever felt safer or happier or more worry-free than we did during those years when my father was so concerned about money.

Our dad stormed through the door to Billy's room looking like King Kong. "Billy, what do you do with your sandwiches?"

Billy was not that stubborn and knew when it was time to talk.

"I give them to this *clochard* who sleeps at the metro stop near my school."

"Why?"

He thought for a while. "Candida makes lousy sam-wiches," he said.

"I can believe that," our dad said. Every time we watched him eat his hamburger at lunch, he complained that Candida flattened it with the spatula while it was cooking and made all the juice run out. He said he'd demonstrated for her a number of times, but she just refused to do it properly. "Maybe she does it on purpose," he'd reflect, making a disgusted face. One day he'd shouted, "THIS IS A FUCKING HOCKEY PUCK!" and side-armed the hamburger into the wall. It bounced off and landed on the floor without breaking apart or leaving a stain.

Seeing that our dad wasn't going to start yelling about the sandwiches, Billy went on more enthusiastically.

"Plus everybody's else comes in this little box, see, with drawings on it?" He made a box of the approximate size with his hands. "And everybody's else has that flat bread like we had in America and peanut butter and jelly and chips and stuff. Sometimes tunafish with mayonnaise and stuff."

"What does Candida give you?"

"Scramble eggs with butter and sometimes ham with butter on a baguette. The scramble eggs leaks on the bread and it's all mushy. Plus I look like a Frog with samwiches like that."

"Well, goddamn it, why didn't you say something before?"

Now Billy shrugged, staring at the floor. "I didn't want Candida to get mad."

"Well, Marcella," our dad turned to our mom, "we're just going to have to go to the commissary and get peanut butter and all the rest of that American crap."

From that moment on, Billy's Americanization pro-ceeded with very few hitches.

* * *

I have never understood why things happen when they do; I don't truly know why we stayed in France for fifteen years and then left everyone behind, including Candida. We "came home" and bought the house on Long Island with the money we'd gotten for selling the one in Paris. It was exactly as our father had predicted: close enough to New York for our mother and far enough away for him. We learned to set the table, wash dishes, pick up after ourselves, but not without a good deal of complaining. It was quite simple: Either we did the dishes and cleaned up after ourselves or didn't get to do anything else. After meals, our father seriously but good-humoredly gave us the Army KP white-glove treatment. He went over the counters with his index finger and if he found a spot or a crumb, we had to start all over again.

The move to America combined with his failing health caused my father to open up about his family in a way he never had before. Up until then, we'd only known that he had left and joined the Army at eighteen, and had never gone home. Now he was longing for his brother and sister, who had both died of bad hearts.

One day I was walking around the property with him. The sky seemed tired and colorless and the land was frozen so that the grass crackled when you stepped on it. All the leaves had fallen while he'd been in the hospital. He was telling me about all the things he wanted to do to the house, where he'd put in a pool and a grape arbor the following spring. Then he started telling me about his sister, Charlotte-Anne, who had died at twenty-five. "You know," he said, "Charlotte-Anne and I used to fight. We had terrible, terrible fights. I was jealous because my mother babied her—she hated me, my mother, because I wouldn't feel sorry for her and thought she was full of shit. My mother died while I was in the Army in Hawaii and I didn't even ask for leave. When Charlotte-Anne died I was thirty years old and we'd never really made up. Never talked about things. All my life it's the one thing I've regretted. She'll never know that I really did love her. That's why I hate it so much when you and Billy fight."

I was blinded by tears; he put his arm around my shoulder and told me not to cry. He said the good thing was there was so much time left in my life for me to be nice to Billy.

I also don't know why he and my mother chose one particular icy, windy February night, as we sat across from each other at the long oak table that had come all the way from Paris with the rest of our furniture, to tell me the story of Billy's birth.

That night at dinner, my parents had drunk a good deal of wine. My father had just finished a particularly difficult chapter of his book and we were celebrating, although he really was not supposed to drink alcohol, even wine.

Billy had gone off to bed hours before; he was going through the worst of what our father called his "growing-up stage." We must have been talking about this "stage" of Billy's in one way or another, when my father suddenly leaned across the table toward me and said, "I want to tell you something, but you have to swear to God never to tell anyone."

My heart froze. I thought he was going to bring up his will.

"I swear," I said, my anxiety rising with my voice.

"See," my father started gently, "I've been offering to tell Billy about his parents for years now. But he doesn't want to know. I keep telling him that if he wants to know, all he has to do is ask.

"So I don't want you ever telling anyone until Billy knows and says it's okay. One day I'll be gone, and maybe he'll ask you."

My mother's face went expressionless then, took on the serene flatness of a mask.

"We were so scared," she whispered. "Every month for the first year a government official came to look in on us. And we thought Billy's mother was going to change her mind and take him away. It was all so damn *illegal*. You see, in France you're not allowed to adopt if you already have a child, and to top it off, we were Americans."

"His parents aren't dead?" I asked, completely bewildered.

"Now, Marcella, will you let me tell this story?" my father said calmly. She had a habit of throwing the end in before the middle, which infuriated us all.

"No, they're not dead," my father said.

I wasn't angry at them; I felt privileged in an odd way. I

had a fleeting sense that this was a once-in-a-lifetime shot, that by tomorrow they would discuss having told me and probably regret it.

"We never met his father but we met his mother," my father said. "I begged his mother after a year to allow us to try to adopt him. See, she wasn't sure she wanted to give him up. She was fifteen when he was born. *Fifteen years old.*" He paused, as though it were still hard for him to comprehend this. "Your age," he said soberly.

I squirmed in my seat but he went right on.

"She came from a very upper-class family and they carted her off somewhere to have the baby. But she refused to give him up for adoption, God knows why. Stubbornness or something.

"The French couple who fostered him the first two years were from the same kind of background. Upper-class and so on, but he was a writer and that's how I knew him. They couldn't have kids. When his wife killed herself he couldn't face raising Billy alone and put him in a children's home. It was up to Billy's real mother to decide what to do."

"I don't understand people like that," my mother said angrily. "How can you give up a child just like that, just because your wife kills herself?"

"We offered to take him immediately, as soon as we found out, but it took another six months for the government to agree. It was touch and go for those six months. Billy's mother didn't want him in a children's home, but she also didn't want to take him back and it would have taken any family several months to get through the bureaucracy. So we had to convince her to wait.

"Billy had been with us a year when we met her. She was a law student at the Sorbonne. She was a tall, thin girl with light blond hair and a really classically beautiful face. Completely poised, she was. A little cold. You know who she looked like? Catherine Deneuve very young. She said she'd researched me. Read a couple of my novels, in French, of course. She said my writing seemed brutal to her. But honest."

My father laughed; his eyes crinkled up and went out of focus.

My mother put in, "We had her over for tea and made Candida take you kids to the Jardin d'Acclimatation. We told her she couldn't bring you back till dinnertime. . . . If you ever got pregnant you'd tell us right away, wouldn't you?" she added quickly, a moment later, as though the thought had just occurred to her. I didn't say anything and made a face at her, a "don't be ridiculous, Mom" face.

"I begged her to give Billy up for his own good. I swore I'd give him the best life I possibly could," my father said.

"She said, 'A much better life, certainly, than *I* could.'

"A week later she met me in a café and gave me a diary she'd kept while she'd been pregnant. She said maybe it would explain things a little to her son. Maybe it would help him understand where he came from. I've never read it. It's for Billy, if he ever asks. If he ever asks you, Channe, the diary is in the vault and has Billy's name on it. But you're not to touch it. Not until Billy asks."

From that day on, I looked at Billy in a different way. It was a bit like learning the root of a word you think you've known forever. You think you know something so well and then suddenly you find out it was something completely different all along. Like the word "cowboy." For years I'd thought it was "calboy." Cow-boy, someone finally told me. Cow-boy. But what did those guys riding horses and carrying pistols and chasing Indians have to do with cows?

I kept my promise to my parents, and never brought the subject up with Billy.

In my life, up until the following spring, I'd had only one encounter with death. I was in eighth grade at the École Internationale Bilingue, when in the middle of October, my best friend Janet Morgan's father died of stomach cancer. He'd been sick a long time. When I'd go over to Janet's to play, she'd knock on her father's bedroom door and I'd go in and shake hands with him in the semi-darkness. The room smelled like a hospital, the close air was heavy with medicine and body smells. Her father did not look like a human being to me, he was so thin and pale and old.

The day after he died, Janet came to school and played

soccer as usual during recreation, ate lunch with us as usual in the cafeteria, laughed as she always did at silly jokes, and sang her favorite Elton John songs aloud in the hallways. Sally, my other best friend, and I (grown-up creatures that we were!) were horrified by Janet's lack of feeling and decorum, and whispered disapprovingly behind her back.

As Fate will have it, the day before my father died, another girl called Janet drove me to the hospital after school, to visit him. Keith kept trying to help but I avoided him because the emotional level he demanded from me was too high. It was late spring and the air was light with those happy sounds. The sun beat hard and yellow through the windshield. The radio was blasting some hip tune. I felt relatively unperturbed by things, not believing for a second that my father was going to die. Janet said, "I wish my father was in the hospital instead of yours."

"God, how could you say a thing like that?" I said.

"I'm serious. Bastard beats us where it doesn't show. I hope he dies a long slow miserable fucking death."

She lifted her shirt and showed me an enormous black bruise on her ribs, turned her head and stared at me blankly through her glasses, her small face pale, her mouth a purplish knot.

This was on my mind when I went into the glass room to see my father. We talked only about Janet and what I could do to help her. My father said short of calling the police, there was nothing we could do. He said if I called the police, Janet's father would probably beat her worse and nothing would come of it. He had that same fatalistic tone in his voice, and I felt completely helpless. I thought, when he gets home, I'll bring Janet over and he'll talk to her. He'll fix everything.

All night I could not get Janet and her father off my mind and kept envisioning the sordid scene. It would play itself out like a film—Janet's father raising his heavy fists—and my intestines would cramp up and come to my throat as though I were riding downhill in a speeding car without brakes.

The next day, Billy and I sat huddled together in the

hospital waiting room while our father fought through his last hours.

"Can you believe this shit? Janet's father beats her!" I must have said this a hundred times, as though it were the only thing that mattered in the world.

"What should I do? Billy, what should I do?"

He watched me with heavy, worried eyes, eyes brimming with tears that refused to fall.

When the end came I went into a fit of hysterical laughter that wouldn't stop. It wouldn't stop after one ten-milligram Valium so the doctor gave me another. He offered Billy one too, but he refused to take it.

During the summer, none of us could face each other. Keith and I broke up; I had no emotions left for anyone. Family friends came and went, taking turns standing vigil over our mother. She had sunk into an alcoholic stupor that withdrew her completely from us and from the world. I despised her for no clear reason, although I told myself it was because she was the most self-indulgent person I'd ever known. "You don't have a right to behave this way," I'd tell her, standing over her prostrate form on the living room couch.

"You're a monster," she'd say in a high-pitched, childish voice. "You have no feelings for anyone except yourself!"

I stopped eating completely and went out to bars every night and stayed in them until they closed. It was incredible that all of my friends were underage, and all of us drank in bars, and no one seemed to care.

And during all of this, alone in his room and alone in our garden pruning the bushes and trees, in three months Billy grew into a tall, slender, strong, and handsome young man.

Very late one night at the end of August, I was so drunk I drove my father's car home with the windows down. The chill of fall was already in the air and suddenly I became aware that my fear had come to visit and was taking up all the space in the car.

I started thinking about the two Janets. Soon after her father died, the first Janet started making up stories that were so horrifying we couldn't even imagine where they'd come from—she told everyone I'd slept with my brother, and that Sally's father had affairs and that Sally's mother had tried to slit her wrists. On and on.

And now, at parties, the second Janet was suddenly getting gang-banged by three or four football players at a time. Anyone who'd give her a beer or smile at her could get her out to a parked car. Pain never shows the way you expect it to. First you run.

When I was very drunk, as I was at that moment, my mind suddenly fed me a single, agonizingly clear picture: my father's green eyes fogging over, staring up at the ceiling while his knuckles turned white in my mother's hand, and me laughing, laughing and not being able to stop.

I started to scream "Why?" as loud as I could. I knew that the next morning, sober, I'd try to bring the image back but it would never come.

So much time was going to pass, so much time before it was going to be all right. And then it hit me that maybe it was really never going to be all right.

Panic-stricken, I stumbled up the stairs of our house to Billy's room and banged on his door. "What? What?" he called out in a confused, sleepy voice.

"It's me!" I cried.

"Come in," he mumbled.

I sat at the edge of his bed in the darkness as I had so many nights as a child. I tried to start out calmly but no words would come, just tears, hot ones smelling of vodka.

"Help me, Billy," I managed.

After a long silence, he said in a gentle, quiet voice, "I can't. I wish to God I could but I can't."

He stared at me with a tight, sad expression while I wept. After a long while it subsided, and Billy said, "I can't stand it either. Stay here with me if you want." He moved over in his double bed.

In a few minutes he was snoring in the loud, nasal way that used to drive me crazy when we'd had to share rooms traveling. But that night the sound was as comforting as a lullaby. I slept without dreams and when I awakened the next morning, he was gone.

On his prompting, we began to go out together to the local hangouts. My girlfriends thought he was beautiful and asked me where I'd been hiding him. They told me there was something about the way he carried his head, about the look in his eye, that they would have known he was my brother immediately, even if he'd walked in alone.

One night Billy asked me out of nowhere, "What was the last thing Daddy said to you?"

We were sitting way in the back of a disco, away from the music and the crowd. The light was dark and reddish on my brother's face and his large eyes seemed particularly bright. The question caught me off guard, and I might have seemed overly ready to respond; I was always grateful when he allowed us to share confidences.

"He told me I was much smarter than I thought and that I shouldn't let any guy talk me into getting married before I was ready."

Billy turned his beer upside down in his mouth and then gazed at me with a blank expression. His mouth began to twitch just slightly; he looked away.

"He told me to take care of the house," Billy said. "'The house,' he said. 'Don't let the house fall apart. If you start with that, keeping the garden and the house in good shape, everything will be all right.'"

"You're doing that," I said enthusiastically, putting my hand over his. "The house is beautiful and so's the garden."

He removed his hand and waved to the waitress for a new round of drinks.

* * *

Within days of taking down the photographs of our father, the beau built a six-foot-tall chicken wire fence around the most glorious section of Billy's garden. The beau wanted to keep his emus from running away. Emus run forty miles an hour and destroy everything in their path. Australian farmers shoot them on sight. They decimated Billy's lilac bushes, roses, and hydrangeas. Our mother acted as though this were amusing, but I wasn't convinced she thought so at all. When something upsets her badly, she finds a way to joke about it. Letting the beau move in and take over was probably her way of defying our father's ghost.

"That bastard," she used to say to me as we drove together through sunsets or moonlit nights, "I can't look at such beautiful sights anymore." And she'd burst into silent tears.

I believed she would have let the beau throw everything that reminded her of our father out the window, including us. But I also believed her hope in this new romance was an enemy in disguise, much closer to despair than a void of emotion.

During the week before Billy's naturalization, I thought about our childhood the way one might be inspired to spring-clean one's dusty memories before the wedding or graduation of a close friend. If there had been a party for him and I'd had to make a toast, I would have told these stories about him as a little boy. But it was to be a solitary event, just the two of us and four hundred immigrants pledging allegiance to the Flag.

It was a particularly hot October morning in New York, even at that early hour. Billy was in his banker's suit and I wore a blue linen dress and high-heeled shoes. All the soon-to-be citizens were in their Sunday clothes, sporting cameras and surrounded by their entire families— grandparents, husbands, wives, children, and grandchildren. We stood in a long line outside the courthouse and everyone smiled at each other with proud, congratulatory expressions. An hour later we approached a desk where Billy was to sign in and receive his papers.

"Willhelm Willich?" said the Puerto Rican clerk.

"No, William Willis," Billy said.

She smiled as though she understood his zeal perfectly well.

"Sign here, Mister Willich."

Billy turned red to the tips of his ears. I began to feel the need to cry but checked myself as Billy would certainly have disapproved.

The courtroom was packed with people from every corner of the world. Most of them were slowly mouthing the words on the pamphlet they'd been handed, entitled "How to Be a Good Citizen," or some such thing. Billy and I read the pamphlet together, leaning toward each other, shoulders touching. "These people are going to raise monsters!" he said between his teeth, pointing to a line about how important it was to raise your children in the drug-free, alcohol-free, rock 'n' roll–free American Way.

The judge was a second-generation Italian, Francesco Giuseppe Antonio Esperanza. In a heavy Brooklyn accent, he talked about his parents' trip over on the boat and their arrival at Ellis Island and how much more room there used to be a century ago for capitalist-minded entrepreneurs. "But it's still America!" he shouted. "Your kids can still make it big, look at me." Everyone laughed. He closed with, "I congratulate you all from the bottom of my heart on this momentous occasion."

Then we all stood up and faced the Flag. "I pledge allegiance," we all began. It seemed that everyone was reading from the pamphlet except Billy and me and the judge. I glanced at my brother quickly out of the corner of my eye and saw his proud chin raised high, his glassy eyes staring straight ahead, and all at once the tears welled up in my throat and came pouring out of my eyes in a most conspicuous way. He elbowed me gently in the ribs. "Don't," he said.

We came out into the bright sunlight a little after noon.

"You want to have lunch somewhere?" Billy suggested in an offhanded way. I readily agreed, having taken the whole day off.

"You cried," he said dead-seriously. "You promised you wouldn't."

Flustered, I apologized, and his face broke into an open, childish smile. "Willhelm Willich, can you believe it?"

It turned out that Billy had made reservations in a very expensive French restaurant near Wall Street. The atmosphere was festive, people were drinking and it was loud and crowded and bright. We had Escargots de Bourgogne followed by sole Meuniere, our favorite dishes as children, which we would invariably order when our parents took us out for Sunday lunch. We each had two glasses of wine.

We talked easily, about our jobs and avoiding the subject of our mother.

"Have a *tarte aux framboises* for dessert, like you used to," I coaxed him.

"On my birth certificate," he said in a matter-of-fact way, "it says *unemployed* next to my mother's name. I figure she was either very rich or very poor."

I drank my wine down to the bottom and nearly choked on it.

"Are you just speculating, or are you asking me?"

"No, no. Tell me."

"What do you want to know?"

"Everything." He shrugged complacently. "Whatever you know."

I repeated almost verbatim the conversation I'd had with my parents late that February night, long ago. Billy gazed at me earnestly, sometimes nervous, sometimes uncomfortable, but he listened without flinching until I got to the end, to the diary that was still lying in the vault, in an envelope with his name on it.

"Do you want to read it?"

He thought about this for a while. His *tarte aux framboises* arrived and he picked at it with the tip of his fork.

"No," he said finally. "You read it. Maybe one day I'll ask you what it says. I don't think so, though. I only have two parents. And I only have one sister."

"Remember how you used to get the raspberries all over your face and I used to get so mad?" I laughed lightly, feeling a warmth spreading upwards from my chest.

"You were such a bitch," he said.

"If you ever want to find her, you know, well, I'd go with you. We could just go knock on her door."

"No," he said flatly. "Thanks."

We were so different. If it had been my mother, I would have wanted to go. But he was exactly the same as he'd always been. He'd made up his mind about it, probably when he first saw his birth certificate. That must have been almost four years earlier, when he'd put his papers in for naturalization. He'd never mentioned it to anyone. Now he apparently knew as much as he wanted to know. I didn't understand it, but I respected his decision.

There were so many things I wanted to tell him, but I had a knot in my throat and tears in my eyes, and he still despised displays.

I looked closely at his face and saw the tiny scars my nails had left on his cheeks during my childish fits of rage.

"Remember when you used to sit on my face and fart?" I asked him. He turned automatically to see if anyone was listening and then burst into a high-pitched giggle.

With a new burst of courage, I said, "Remember that night I came into your room hysterical after Daddy died?"

"Yeah," he said, and stared at his tarte.

"I think you saved me. I'm sorry I was such a bitch when we were little, Billy."

He shrugged this off. "Kids are kids, after all, aren't they? It wasn't easy for you either."

THE DIARY

Translated from the French by
Charlotte-Anne Willis; October, 1988

Thursday 24 of June, 1960. Paris.

Aunt Susanne gave me this little diary and said I should
write down my thoughts. That I may not want to now but in
years to come I'll thank her for it, the way I will for the piano
lessons.

I'm already happy I didn't give up the piano but what
difference does it make now? What difference does anything make and who am I dear God and what did I ever do
to deserve this? That is my thought for today.

Friday 25 of June.

Well, the cruise left this morning. Mother canceled for
both of us two days ago. She says she couldn't possibly leave
me at a time like this. Everything with her and Aunt Susanne
has become "at a time like this," like they're talking about a
national disaster and not something that is my fault personally.

Mother wanted to go to Greece so badly. I could see it
in her eyes. She probably thought she'd meet a potential
husband on the cruise. I can just imagine how she pictured
him: a man wearing a linen suit with a little ascot and a pair
of binoculars around his neck. He's the one leaning on the
railing of the de Brieux's one-hundred-and-fifty-meter yacht
reciting Greek poetry in Greek into the wind.

Saturday 26 of June.

She's starting to get on my nerves with this cruise. It's all
she talks about. How upset she is that she had to cancel on

such short notice. How the de Brieux are never going to forgive her and how they are not people you want to offend. She walks around in circles wringing her hands and rubbing her eyelids. Aunt Susanne keeps telling her to calm herself, to be quiet. I have nowhere to go. That's Rule Number One around here now: I have to hide inside till they can figure out where to send me. So I have to be with them all day long in a way I've never had to be in my life.

I said, "Mother why don't you just have a car drive you down to Marseille and join them?"

"No, no, no don't be a silly girl. I'm your mother aren't I? What kind of mother would I be if I left you at a time like this?"

The same kind you've always been, I wanted to say. I didn't say anything as usual because there's really no point in making things worse.

That habit she has of rubbing her eyelids with her fingertips has gotten out of control. And now she's biting all her nails off again after she'd gotten it down to biting only two. That took her ten years and now because of me all that hard work is lost.

Her eyelids are red, her eyes are big and round and when she sits there hunched over biting her nails she looks like this exotic monkey from Africa I saw at the Jardin des Plantes.

Aunt Susanne says Mother is fragile. Too fragile and that this might really send her over the edge. Don't think I don't feel totally responsible because I do.

But my thought for today is this: Nothing's going to change between Mother and me even now because she's the kind of person who bends with the wind and I think she doesn't have a personal thought in her head. It's Grandmother's fault, that's the truth, because Grandmother controls the money. But look where that got us!

Sunday 27 of June.

Mother told Grandmother, my three uncles, my oldest aunt, my brother, all my cousins, and the de Brieux that I

151

have a thyroid problem. I'm going to spend the summer in a sanatorium by the sea. I got sick so suddenly that it was a shock to everyone. That's why we had to turn down the cruise on such short notice. Aunt Susanne must have made up the story because Mother doesn't have that kind of an imagination.

I respect Aunt Susanne because she's not really like the rest of the family. She's made money on her own with Saint Laurent and she doesn't have to put up with Grandmother's nonsense like the rest of them. Aunt Susanne says she's the only one of Grandmother's offspring who has testicles. The brothers are all eunuchs, she says. I looked that word up in the dictionary and it made me laugh.

But the inheritance is nothing to laugh at and even Aunt Susanne will honestly tell you this herself. She still wants to be included and when she stands against Grandmother and the rest of them it's always "to make a point" and it's always temporary.

This time it's not about one of their silly secret love affairs that the entire family hears about within two days anyway. This time no one must ever find out. No one must find out. No one must find out. How many times have I heard that in the last five days? About a million. Mother had to tell Aunt Susanne the truth because she couldn't cope with it herself.

They say we have to lie to protect my future. They say it has absolutely nothing to do with the inheritance. I think they're hypocrites.

Monday 28 of June.

"Think productively, that's what I do." Aunt Susanne says this all the time. She's of course the one who found the apartment in Trouville. It's not too far from Paris so Mother and Aunt Susanne can drive up whenever they want. They say the sea air will do me good. That's a good one considering I'm not allowed to go outside. I'll have a phone so I can call them anytime. And it goes with the story because if

I was in a sanatorium they couldn't stay with me anyway. We're going to Trouville tomorrow morning.

I'm scared. I had the best grades in my class. I was the best in French and music and history and some of the other girls did much worse things. For example my friend Sophie slept with the priest who was our biology instructor.

Why me? That's what I don't understand.

Tuesday 29 of June. Trouville.

Night.
They left at nine to miss the traffic. Now I'm alone. I don't mind. The *autoroute* was completely blocked outside Paris and the gas fumes made me sick. I threw up out the back window of Aunt Susanne's Fiat. I thought the roof was caving in. I'm not claustrophobic or at least I've never been until now. I told them I had to throw up so Aunt Susanne pulled off the road. They both stared at me as though they thought it might already be time or something.

"What's wrong? What's wrong?" Mother pulled my hair away from my forehead and made a disgusted face. Poor Mother, she never changed one of our diapers and never saw us vomit so it must really have come as a shock.

"Oh God, Susanne do you think—"

"Don't be completely ridiculous, Sylvie."

Mother started rubbing her eyelids, going round and round with the tips of her chewed-up fingers.

"If you start being completely neurotic then she'll get frightened and goddamn it, Sylvie, I'm not going to put up with your nerves today."

Aunt Susanne can really say what she means at times.

Maybe to them I'm a dog. People talk to a dog. "Cute doggie," they say. "Aren't you just the cutest doggie in the world!" and then the dog wags its tail so they figure it understands everything. But then five minutes later they'll turn around and say something nasty about the dog to a guest or something, *right in front of the dog!* like, "When I bought this dog I had no idea the breed was so stupid." It doesn't make sense.

Wednesday 30 of June.

Of course, Mother immediately began to complain about the room to the concierge. Mother was embarrassed by me so she acted haughty to the concierge. She always does that. I think the room is very nice. Mother said she thought the room would be much bigger. The concierge explained in a gentle voice that it's the only one available with its own bathroom and kitchen.

The concierge is red-faced and fat and sweet. She didn't even throw me a second look.

Once the concierge went back downstairs Mother started pacing and wringing her hands.

"Why? WHY?" she said. Aunt Susanne was standing by the window staring out at the street.

"Oh, look! You can see a bit of the harbor from here," she said.

"WHY, damn it? What I simply cannot comprehend is WHY she didn't tell us before it was too late!"

"What's done is done." She was trying to sound calm but I could tell she was getting angrier by the second. "So just shut up, will you?"

"My God! Fifteen, Susanne! FIFTEEN! Think about it. Her whole life is ahead of her! But really, what did I do? I sent my children to the best schools, I taught them everything I knew . . ."

"Here, have a cognac and sit down. Calm yourself, Sylvie. Calm yourself."

Mother started to cry. After she stopped crying she sat down next to me on the bed where I was lying facing the wall and took my hand.

"My darling baby. My poor poor darling baby. I hate to leave you like this. I'll stay with you, how's that?"

"It would be better if you went back to Paris with Susanne," I told her.

Thursday 1 of July.

Mother makes me laugh. Grandmother could tell her to go piss off the balcony of her loge at the opera and Mother would do it without blinking an eye.

Friday 2 of July.

Night.
The apartment is not bad at all. In the main room the walls, the bedspread, the wood table, and the wicker chairs are all white. Like in a sanatorium. The shutters on the two big windows are also white. There's too much light in here unless I close them and when I close them it's too hot. But one thing I can't stand is the sun pouring in all day long from seven in the morning till eight at night screaming BEACH! CRUISE! LIFE! in my ears.

It's not bad, being alone. Better than those five days between the time I told them and they brought me here which were the worst days of my life up until now. I'm sure there's worse yet to come, however.

I spent the whole day in bed staring at the ceiling. I thought maybe I'll get up and write in my diary but I couldn't seem to do it. Maybe I'll draw in my sketchbook but I couldn't do that either. Things only seem to become okay when the sun goes down.

The groceries are here so the concierge must have come up. I don't remember letting her in. Maybe I'm losing my sense of reality?

Maybe I need a piano. I'll ask them to bring me a piano and then I'll probably lie in bed and stare at it.

Sunday 4 of July.

Mother came on Saturday and stayed until this morning. Her eyelids are even redder than usual. Her eyes are washed out. They used to sparkle a weird blue sort of like the Mediterranean with the sun on it. She's not happy and she says she doesn't sleep. I don't know if she sleeps or not at home but here I don't sleep and I know that she did because I watched her. She didn't move once all night.

She says she's worried about me but I think she's more worried because she's getting older and isn't attracting the kind of men she's used to attracting. I say good, because the kind of men she's used to attracting should be shot. How old was I when my father left? Four, I guess. He ran away with a model, "that young floozie" Mother says. He doesn't care about being a father and that's fine with me. I don't remember how old I was when Mother started with the men. It was like this. One guy would be a painter and then suddenly painting was the most important thing in her life. Suddenly we had new, modern paintings hanging on every inch of wall space at home, paintings that looked like someone had flung shit at a white canvas from across the room. The next guy would be a married bomb scientist and suddenly physics was crucial, how the Americans really aren't that much further ahead than the Russians and here we are a little country stuck in the middle, we have to protect ourselves, etc. She had one South American revolutionary who was about twenty-two and had long greasy hair and a beard and during him she hung a poster of Marx in the bathroom.

She forgot about Marx and then one day Grandmother came to tea. Grandmother saw the poster of Marx and threatened to disinherit the whole bunch of us and Mother took the poster down immediately.

You didn't have time to get used to one man before a new one would arrive. I don't know what it is with Mother but she always manages to pick men who really love to talk about themselves. Mother acts like they're the world's greatest genius but she hides every single one of them from Grandmother.

The one thing you can count on with Mother is that Beauty and Class are the most important things on earth and that you should be friends with People of Importance even if they're assholes.

I don't give a damn about the men but I wish she'd get a clue about her feelings. Why am I different from her? Why couldn't I be the same and not think so much? My brother is different too, but in a different way than me.

Monday 5 of July.

I've been thinking about my brother. He's left for Germany already with Pierre-Antoine. It's funny when I think about them traveling and laughing and so on and here I am.

I wouldn't be honest if I didn't say that my brother is like a brick wall. A very handsome brick wall with lots of brick-wall type of opinions. When you're a boy raised without a father I suppose you think if you act sweet or girlish or weak in any way they'll call you a fag, so you compensate. He's like a Nazi with his opinions—I think that's a reaction to Mother being like a blade of grass in the wind. But I couldn't be sure.

I'm not sorry for writing this.

If I die they'll find this and say, "My God, we had no idea Véronique was such an angry child! That nice quiet girl."

That is my thought for tonight.

Tuesday 6 of July.

5 P.M.: Mother just called and said she's coming up to spend the night. She'll open the shutters and say let's get some fresh sea air in here and now I'll have to pretend to sleep at night and I'm tired of pretending.

Wednesday 7 of July.

Night. I can't sleep again. Maybe I'll write so much this'll turn into a book like *The Diary of Anne Frank* that we had to read last spring. Except I don't think I'm going to die. I'll record everything anyway. They say Françoise Sagan was seventeen when she wrote *Bonjour Tristesse*, so maybe there's hope for me. I always did win first prize for essays in French class. They told me I had a brilliant imagination. I swear to God a person couldn't invent what's happened to me.

So Mother arrived with more dopey clothes. Lots of flowers and polka-dots and so on. Horrible. She brought some novels (I haven't looked at them, who could read at a time like this?). We played backgammon until pretty late. I won four games in a row and then I said, "It's no fun, you're not paying attention."

She sat back in her wicker chair and started rubbing her eyelids. "Does it hurt?"

"Don't rub your eyelids like that," I told her.

"Oh." She stared down at her hands like she didn't recognize them at all. Then she smiled at me, but she looked about to cry. It's the strangest thing. I've wanted her to cry over me for years, to come to some realizations concerning the fact that I exist and have feelings too, but now when she looks about to cry I hate it.

"I want a piano, Mother," I said in a cold tone, imitating Phillippe. When he wants something he just says it like this, "Mother, now don't say a word, I've done research on this matter and have found that the best mode of transportation for me at this time is a motorbike." Whatever it is, he gets it. Mother melts like a Camembert in the sun when Phillippe talks like that.

"A piano? All right, darling. We'll get you a little piano. What else can I get you? Anything. Ask me for anything."

"I want curtains. The shutters closed make the room too hot. White ones."

"All right," she said, looking unsure. "You want to keep the air circulating, you know."

I didn't say anything.

"All right," she said. "Anything else?"

"Make this go away. All of it."

She sighed, slapped her knees and got up. She poured herself a cognac in the kitchen and brought it back. We sat in silence for a long time, staring at the corners.

In the morning she opened the shutters and made

158

scrambled eggs. She's the worst cook on earth but I ate her eggs to make her happy and then I threw up. She washed me and then puffed the pillows on the couch where she slept and watered the plants that I already watered yesterday.

Thursday 8 of July.

I am pretending the world outside doesn't exist. Sometimes it's easy and sometimes it's not. It's not when Mother is here. Today it's raining and that helps because I don't feel like I'm missing out on life. I've decided that if I want to sleep all day and stay up all night I can. I'll burn the red candles on the table and stare at the corners wondering if I'll ever be normal again. They say things pass. You get over them. Yes, if they stop existing in your mind. Like old school friends who move away. But how can something like this stop existing in your mind? It will always exist and I'm starting to hurt all the time now, which only reminds me that it will always exist. I feel like I swallowed a magic seed and now a watermelon is sitting low in my intestines, growing and blocking everything.

I feel ripe, like an over-ripe pear that's starting to get moldy. I lie here and think this can't be me. My God, I think, what if my brother could see me now? He'd probably kill Pierre-Antoine, just on principle even though they're best friends.

I hate this thing and would like to kill it. I know this isn't normal and I know that if I fell out the window or something I would probably die too. Do I want to die? Or worse, be crippled forever? No. I know I'm not normal because they say I'm supposed to feel some kind of love for it. But I don't, I feel sorry, but that isn't love, is it? I don't love anything or anyone.

Saturday 10 of July.

Aunt Susanne came with a manual to help Mother hang the curtains today. They finally had to call the concierge's son because they were scared to climb the ladder. They wouldn't leave the boy alone. They stood at the foot of the ladder in their silk dresses and high-heeled shoes and gave him advice, as if they knew how to hammer a nail into a wall!

Every time they called him "my pet" I cringed. He didn't say a word and neither did I. He kept looking at me though, over his shoulder. I was lying on the bed staring at the ceiling. He's about seventeen, tall and thin, so thin it looks like he grew too fast. He has saggy shoulders and big eyes that seem surprised by everything in the world. Or maybe it's just me that surprises him.

Mother said to Aunt Susanne, "Do you think it's all right for him to see her?" nodding sideways at me.

"What do you think—you pay his mother a thousand francs a month to keep her."

The boy kept on hammering. That's how they are in my family: Nobody cares about insulting the intelligence of peons and dogs.

It's true that money takes care of everything. His mother can probably use the thousand francs a month. Plus I wonder how much they paid to get the phone installed. Most people wait a year. In any case, Aunt Susanne rented the place under a fake name to make sure no one ever finds out.

They left before dinner because there was a big fête at Saint Laurent they had to go to.

Sunday 11 of July.

Outside in the street there are lots of children and grown-ups walking, holding hands, and laughing. Sundays are a family holiday and it makes me want to throw up. I wish they'd all go home instead of parading their happiness in front of my window.

Tuesday 13 of July.

Aunt Susanne came late yesterday afternoon and stayed overnight. I wasn't expecting her, especially on a Monday.

She said she thought it would cheer me up. We played backgammon for a franc a point until midnight. I lost ten francs. She said I didn't owe her when I tried to pay. It's all their money anyway, money they left me to give the concierge if I want anything.

By that time Susanne had drunk half the bottle of Williamine she'd brought with her. Her chignon was beginning to come apart and she kept sticking pieces of hair back in with her fingers. She was red in the face and her eyes were all shiny.

"You're very grown-up for your age," she said. "You had to grow up fast, I suppose, because you certainly didn't get much help from your mother." I think Aunt Susanne feels guilty because it happened at her birthday party that Grandmother threw at the Château in November.

"Now you're going to be a grown-up woman before your time. Poor baby. Your mother is my favorite sister, you know that. She's had a fragile nature since she was born. I've protected her all her life and I don't know where she'd be without me. It's them, you understand, the others. They'd crucify us if they knew. You understand that, don't you? She loves you very much even though she doesn't know how to show it very well. Do you believe that?"

"I don't care." I stared at her with a flat expression through the candlelight.

"Don't be ridiculous. Of course you care."

No one said anything for a while and we listened to a drunk out in the street crying about how nobody loved him.

"It hurt her much more than anyone knows when your papa left. Your grandmother and everyone else were completely against that marriage. But since he was from a good family—well . . . You know how it is with fashion photographers, they like those young girls. The man isn't in one city long enough to make a phone call to his children. The bastard. We tried to get him but he's in Northern Iceland shooting for the winter line. The bastard."

Aunt Susanne got up and went to the window. She put her hands on her hips and arched her back. She pulled the curtain to the side and looked out at the street.

"Why didn't you tell us before it was too late? My God,

you really waited till the last possible minute. We could have taken you to England. Were you afraid of us?"

"I already told you I didn't know."

"But how could you not know?" She spun around and looked me straight in the eye.

"I didn't think it was possible, you know." I stared right back at her. "Because nothing happened between us. Nothing like they said it was going to be."

Aunt Susanne snorted. "And what did they say it was going to be like?"

"Different than that. I'm telling you nothing happened."

"Well obviously *some*thing happened."

She waited, I didn't say anything, so she let it drop. Thank God they are not a talkative bunch in my family when it comes to these things.

Wednesday 14 of July.

Bastille Day and I'm alone. Right now, let's see—Pierre-Antoine and Phillippe are doing Germany by Eurail. Mother and Aunt Susanne are at the Comtesse de Merde's château for a fête and Grandmother is in St. Tropez with the rest of the grandchildren. The fireworks will start soon and they'll watch from the balcony of the villa that sits up on a hill over the bay and then maybe they'll have a glass of champagne. Maybe they'll drink to me, poor Véronique who's sitting in a sanatorium by the sea with a thyroid problem that has ruined her whole body to say nothing of her life.

Thursday 15 of July.

The strangest thing happened yesterday. While I was drawing in my sketchbook and listening to the drunk people out in the street the concierge's son came up and knocked on the door.

At first I was scared, I couldn't imagine who it could be. I opened the door a crack and looked out.

He was standing out in the hall shuffling his feet and looking guilty. There was a plate covered with wax paper in his hand and it was almost as if he couldn't decide whether to give it to me or not, though that was why, I guess, he was here to begin with.

"I thought—since it's the Fourteenth—well, my mother made this cake and there's a lot left, so I thought—"

"Thank you," I said and took the plate. I thought about closing the door on him but for some reason I stepped away and told him to come in. He looked over his shoulder for a second and then came in, dragging his feet like a kid who's just been sent to the corner of the classroom with the idiot hat.

"Do you want something to drink? There's juice and some Williamine my aunt left."

"Oh, that's okay," he said. I can't stand up too long without getting an ache in my lower back and in my ankles so I sat down on the bed with cushions behind me and told him to sit down on the couch.

The sky was beginning to darken and the shapes in the room were fading into the shadows. I like this time of day.

"Should I turn on the lights?" he asked me.

"No."

"Can you go out? There are fireworks down at the beach in a little while."

"Of course not," I said as though he was the stupidest person in the world. "If I could go out why the hell would I be here instead of in Paris with all my friends and my family?"

"How stupid of me. I'm sorry."

"Well don't be sorry."

I hate myself sometimes. Here I am being nasty to him and he's so kind. Why? Because I need someone to be nasty to and there's no one else around.

"Well. My name's Benoit."

"Véronique."

"Nice to meet you."

"Not under these circumstances," I said.

He waited awhile, looking around guiltily as though he

felt he really shouldn't be prying. I didn't say anything, just watched him with a cold expression.

"I'm sorry you have to be alone so much. It makes me sad."

"I don't need you to feel sorry for me, I can do that myself."

He got up. "I didn't mean to disturb you."

"It's all right."

"Well, goodbye, then."

"Listen, I'm not going anywhere. If you have time, stop by again."

"I will."

"Good."

"Well then. I guess I'll go down to the beach."

It's funny how you can write down exactly what two people say to each other and it doesn't sound at all like the same thing.

Friday 16 of July.

I suppose I should say something about Pierre-Antoine. I mean, if I die they should know what happened. Or didn't happen.

He's Aunt Susanne's first husband's nephew so what does that make him to me? My cousin but not by blood. A good thing that it's not by blood Mother said, because then you could have genetic defects. I would never have gotten to know him beyond the regular family fêtes if he hadn't been my brother's best friend for the past hundred years.

In the family they say Phillippe and Pierre-Antoine's behavior is normal for boys their age and always has been. I don't think so. It's a mutual admiration society from which everyone else is completely excluded except me because I'm no threat, I'm a mascot. I love to watch the older girls try to get in.

When I was ten and they were fourteen they talked in front of me about how they were already *screwing* girls and what they did to them. That's normal too, I guess. But I think they were lying. I think the truth is they're terrified of girls.

Sometimes Pierre-Antoine said that one day he would show me everything so that I would be ready for later on. I couldn't wait.

I learned everything I know from Pierre-Antoine and that isn't much. He'd smile so sweetly and be so warm and tender I was completely taken. The sweetest moments of my adolescence are when he is being nice and paying attention to me.

He taught me how to kiss someone passionately with my mouth open and how to allow someone to touch my breasts and so on. That was before I had breasts. Not that they ever got very big. Except for now where they're so swollen I feel like someone tortured me by filling them up with a tire pump.

One time as a joke my brother called me "you little slut" and I threw a coffee mug at him and broke his nose.

Sunday 18 of July.

I think Pierre-Antoine and Phillippe adore each other because they're like mirror reflections of one another. Oh aren't I beautiful, mirror mirror on the wall! Phillippe is dark and Pierre-Antoine is fair. They both have thin, straight noses and those cold blue eyes. I wonder if they ever kiss or touch each other down there and tell each other I love you.

When I can't sleep I think about all the ways things could have turned out differently, how I should've done this and shouldn't have done that. Now Phillippe's nose has a sort of purplish bump on one side which makes Pierre-Antoine the better looking of the two and that drives my brother crazy. Phillippe keeps his head turned to the side while he's talking to people so that they can't see the bump. I'm sorry I broke his nose because it means so much to him. If it didn't make him look queer I bet he'd ask Mother if he could have plastic surgery.

Mother stayed last night and I don't like to write in front of her or Susanne because maybe they'll get curious and want to know what I think.

165

The piano arrived yesterday afternoon. It's a little white Yamaha from Japan.

Tuesday 20 of July.

Benoit came up yesterday after work. He must work in a pastry shop because he smells like dough. He wanted me to play for him. He says he loves classical music more than anything. So I played him "Für Elise" and then the Moon-light Sonata and he almost fainted he was so thrilled. Then he ran back downstairs and got his record player. It's an antique, I swear. It's a square black thing with speakers built into the sides and a handle so you can carry it. We listened to the *Four Seasons* and I told him that the summer sounds like winter to me and the winter sounds like summer. He said not at all, the summer is hot and violent and the winter is snowy and quiet.

"*This* summer is certainly hot and violent," I told him, and snorted angrily.

That made him nervous so we sat in silence awhile and then he asked me to play the Moonlight Sonata again, which I did.

"God you're good," he said.

"No. Madame Agathe says I'm too lazy to ever be really good."

It was two in the morning when he left. I fell asleep and woke up this morning and wrote this down. My thought for today is this: I like him and I don't care if he's the concierge's son.

Thursday 22 of July.

He does work in a pastry shop. He told me so. He's been up here every night after work. We listen to records and talk about life. He wants to know what I'm going to do after this. I say I don't know, go back to school, I guess. He says one of the books Mother brought is one of his old-time favorites, *Germinal*, by Zola. He says I should read it so I'm reading it. It's about miners before there were unions of any kind. It's horrible. Everybody has babies and they're even younger than me.

Friday 23 of July.

Benoit came by after work and I played him the Moonlight Sonata for the twentieth time since I got the piano. I'm teaching him scales. Do ré mi fa sol la ti do backwards and forwards. He's got good hands for the piano, long and supple, but strong, an unusual combination. He gets nervous when I touch his hands, jumps back like I burned him or something. I guess he's not used to being touched in general. I told him Mother and Aunt Susanne are arriving tomorrow and he won't be allowed to come up till they leave. He says he understands how they feel.

Sunday 25 of July.

The first thing Mother and Aunt Susanne said when they arrived was "Whose record player is that?" as though someone had broken in.

I told them the concierge's son lent it to me. They said why didn't I ask them to bring a good one from Paris?

I said I hadn't thought about it and I liked the way the records sound scratchy on this one. They looked at me as if I was crazy.

"Listen," Aunt Susanne said, "don't get too friendly with that boy. You never know. The things you tell him he could use against us later on."

"What do you mean?"

"Blackmail," she said.

"You're totally ridiculous, Aunt Susanne."

That is the first time I've ever said anything like that to them. We were having lunch and they sat there staring at me. I felt like saying a lot more but didn't.

I like it so much better when they're not here. They try to cheer me up by saying that in the fall everything will be back to normal. I'll go back to school and see all my girlfriends and everything will be fine. Mother says she's bought me some fabulous clothes but she's keeping them as a surprise for when I get home. She says won't my girlfriends be jealous! My girlfriends seem about as far away as the moon.

The only thing that seems real to me is Benoit and *Germinal*. And when it kicks. My God! I swear I saw a fist go by, just like that, under my skin that's stretched tight like a drum. A fist!

Today I'm thinking that I thought I would hate it till the end but I don't hate it anymore. I'm afraid I'll begin to love it and I won't be able to stand what they're going to do. I'm sick of thinking so much.

Monday 26 of July.

Benoit said tonight that he hates priests and organized religion. That was after I told him I went to an all-girls' lycée and that our teachers were nuns and priests. He says that *Germinal* made him interested in socialism so he started to read Marx and then Lenin, even. God, he's so smart. I can't believe how smart he is considering he's the son of the concierge. He says he still hates organized religion but he isn't too big on socialism anymore. He says it's because socialism forces *ethics* and *principles* on you the same way religion does. Or something like that. And no mind should be forced to think by a formula.

"My mother's never read a book in her life but she always tells me to read everything so I can get different opinions, broaden my horizons. You know, she didn't have all the opportunities I'm going to have."

"What does your father do?"

"My father?" He stared at the floor and the tips of his ears turned red. "I have no idea. I've never met him."

Now isn't that something? I guess that throws my philosophy concerning boys who grow up without their fathers.

Wednesday 28 of July.

Benoit asked me today, "Who did that to you?" nodding toward my belly. Who did that to you he said, like I had nothing to do with it.

Well, neither of us did, really.

"An old friend," I told. "My cousin by marriage."

"Does he know?"

I shook my head. "No one knows. No one but you, your mother, my mother, and my aunt."

He didn't say anything.

"You're wondering why a girl like me with every opportunity in the world didn't go to England, right? Because I didn't think it was possible. You know, you study biology and your older brother tells you things. I didn't think it could happen because, excuse me for being vulgar, but I didn't even have sex with the guy."

"But that's impossible."

"That's exactly what *I* thought. You think I'm lying to you."

We looked at each other for a while.

"No," he said.

A miracle. He's the first person who's believed me. He's also the first one who doesn't blame Pierre-Antoine and think he's the Devil incarnate.

Friday 30 of July.

I told him the whole story. Funny, because I've never told it before. No one wanted to know. It's a dirty story. You don't talk about things like that. It didn't seem dirty when I told Benoit. It only seemed sad and stupid. That's what it is, sad and stupid. And that's my thought for today.

169

Sunday 1 of August.

Aunt Susanne brought me mail yesterday. There was a postcard from my brother and a letter from my best friend Anne.

The letter from Anne seemed so stupid to me I could cry. She sent me a sample of her new artwork. A whole bunch of pastel-colored whirls that cover a whole sheet of drawing paper. They remind me of wall decorations in a little girl's bedroom. Clouds and butterflies and sweet thoughts to sleep by. I am so angry I could vomit like a volcano. Anne's letter says she hopes I'll be better soon and that she met a guy on the beach in Biarritz and he keeps trying to kiss her and she keeps pushing him away. She doesn't think it's right to kiss someone before you're engaged. She says that Isabelle wrote her from Provence that Martine has been saying mean things about Anne and me. That we smoked cigarettes behind the school and cheated on the Latin exam.

I couldn't give a shit, I swear to God, about any of their nonsense.

Phillippe writes that he's sorry to hear I'm sick. He says he hopes I get well fast. He says it's too bad about the cruise. He says Pierre-Antoine says hello. Write in care of the French Consulate in Berlin, he says.

I'd like to write him back and say, "Dear Phillippe, I wish you were here to help me but you wouldn't understand."

Or: "Dear Pierre-Antoine and Phillippe, I am alone and so frightened and don't get me wrong, I don't blame Pierre-Antoine at all, but something terrible has happened . . ."

It's a nice thought, but what a lot of trouble and pain it would cause everybody.

Monday 2 of August.

All day long I've been thinking about that stupid day. It was a Saturday. Grandmother invited the whole family to her château for the weekend to celebrate Aunt Susanne's birth-day.

Pierre-Antoine rode down from Paris on his new English motorcycle. All the girl cousins (and boy cousins too) gathered around in a circle to admire it and him. I didn't. I knew he'd show me later. He was wearing a leather jacket with chains on it that he wouldn't take off even inside. The whole house was crowded with people, sitting by fireplaces, playing games like chess and backgammon. Some went riding, some took walks. Everyone was waiting for the big evening fête. Sometime after lunch Pierre-Antoine came up to me during a backgammon game and whispered to me that he wanted to take me for a ride on the motorcycle. He led me out through the kitchen because he wanted it to be a secret.

The fields had been harvested a long time ago and were a darker gray than the sky. There was a wind but it wasn't cold. Pierre-Antoine drove for about half an hour and then stopped by the edge of a forest and said, "Let's take a walk, stretch our legs."

My heart was racing when he took my hand. It was so dark in the woods I couldn't see his face but I could see the wideness of his shoulders in the leather jacket and the curve of his white neck.

"You do know," he said in that tender voice, "that I've been in love with you since you were twelve?"

Every time he's said that to me I've believed him. I doubt it's true but it is a possibility. Because I'm just a baby to him and to Phillippe.

Let me remember. There's no point to lying. He kissed me and slowly pulled me down under a big tree. The ground was damp but the leaves were dry. I was thinking about The Big Moment. I thought maybe he'll be happy, maybe he'll really love me if I let him go all the way with me. I was wearing a wool skirt and he was in jeans. I let him pull my underwear off. He unzipped the jeans and rubbed up against my thigh a little. Just as I thought This Is It, The Big Moment, a warm splotch hit the top of my leg.

He didn't say anything except "Ooops. Damn, I'm sorry."

KAYLIE JONES

I felt happy that for once he wasn't perfect and I thought well, I'll forgive him. "It doesn't matter," I said. I stayed there for a while staring up at the tree, scratching his head lightly, which was on my chest.

After a while he moved away from me. Then he said, "Well, we'd better get back." I wiped the spot away with my underwear and put them in the pocket of my coat. Then we rode back to the château. There was something about sitting up against him with the engine buzzing hard beneath us, my arms around him and my face pressed into the leather jacket that made me really feel I was in love with him and that it didn't matter. I started to wonder if he'd ever really slept with a girl and then I got excited thinking maybe I knew something nobody else did. He dropped me at the kitchen door. The cooks were laughing, banging pots and pans around. He kissed me on the cheek and zoomed around to the front of the house, making pebbles and dust fly.

The next day Pierre-Antoine took my cousin Florence who is eighteen for a ride. They didn't come back until nightfall as we were all getting ready to leave. Florence's face was so pink it looked like they'd been riding really fast into the wind. I decided Pierre-Antoine would have to get down on his knees and beg me before I'd ever let him kiss me again.

I've never had regular periods and for the first three months after that day I had a little blood at about the right time of the month and I thought, I'm finally becoming normal. When I started to get sick to my stomach I thought I had a flu that everyone else at school was having. Later still I started to gain weight and I thought it was from nerves.

Who would ever have thought that something was wrong.

Wednesday 4 of August.

Benoit had the day off so he stayed with me all day. It was raining. I gave him his piano lesson and then we played gin. He beat me about ten times. I told him I'd finished *Germinal*.

172

"Makes you feel you're not the worst off in the world," he said. "I'm glad I was born now instead of last century or I'd be one of those kids working in a factory or a mine."

"Not me," I said. "I'd be married off already to some asshole count or duke."

He thought that was hilarious.

I don't know why but in the middle of his laughing, I started to cry.

"Don't cry," he said in his quiet voice, taking my hand on the tabletop.

"My life is ruined."

"Your life isn't ruined. You've got to make it so that your life isn't ruined. It's up to you."

"I'm never going to be able to tell the truth to anyone. What's going to happen to me later on? I can't ever go to the beach again with these marks! And what if I find a good man someday, what's he going to say when he sees my body scarred up like this?"

"If he's a good man you'll be able to tell him the truth and he won't care a bit."

"You're the only friend I have in the world and in a couple of weeks they'll take me away and I'll never see you again."

"That'll be your choice to make, not theirs."

How incredible that I never thought of that before.

Thursday 5 of August.

I've decided that I won't sign the adoption papers. I've decided to forgive everyone for everything.

Friday 13 of August.

Last Friday, Mother came for the night and ended up staying until this morning. I got sick. I was throwing up and had a fever and pains in my lower stomach. The doctor they paid off came. He said I had the flu but that everything was fine in the other department. I was happy to hear that. I keep thinking about those little fists and feet going by, boom-boom, they're pushing, like, let me out of here already!

After about two days I told Mother I wanted her to go downstairs and tell Benoit to come up and have dinner with us. She said "Are you crazy?" and I said, "No, I'm dead serious."

She thought about it for a while, looking confused, and went down to get him. Benoit had the flu too. He said he'd come up the next evening.

What a nice dinner we had! They talked about the Résistance during the War. He said almost all the leaders of the Résistance were Communists. Benoit said his mother was a big Résistante and hid American pilots in her attic. In fact, he said, his father was probably an American pilot.

"Your father was a Marxist when he was young," Mother said to me, taking my hand. "Did you know that?"

Of course I didn't know that. I don't know anything about him except that he sends us expensive toys at Christmas. Toys! As though we're still ten years old. I don't care. I don't need him anyway.

"I'm going to Paris for university," Benoit suddenly said. "Next year. I want to study law."

"How wonderful!" Mother said, getting all flushed and excited. You'd think he was the son of the Prime Minister the way she was carrying on.

So he started eating with us every night. His mother prepares the dinners and he brings them up and eats with us. His mother is a good cook. Much better than my mother.

This morning, just before Mother left, I told her I wasn't going to sign the adoption papers.

"What!" She looked about to faint and had to sit down.

"Don't worry," I said, "I don't intend to keep it. I just won't give it up for adoption right away. I want to know what's going on. I want to have control if I don't like what I see."

"You're crazy! You're going to make the parents' life miserable! They're going to live in terror that you're going to take it away!"

"I don't give a damn, Mother. Foster parents or I'm telling Grandmother everything."

She started to cry. "You don't have to blackmail me," she said. "I'm your mother. My God, Susanne's going to throw a fit."

"It's not her business." Oh my voice can be so cold. Where did I learn to have such a cold voice?

"It's all my fault!" Mother cried out and put her face down on the table between her arms. "It's all my fault! You were always such a good child, so quiet and thoughtful, never into trouble like your brother." She looked up at me suddenly with a tormented face. "Do you think something's wrong with your brother? Do you think he hates me or something?"

I didn't say anything for a while. "No," I said.

"You were never into trouble like he was. I was never worried about you. I thought you'd take care of yourself."

I said, "Don't be like this now," and patted her head. "Everyone needs their mother, you know, even if they're a good child."

Sunday 15 of August.

Benoit made me swear that I would sign the papers if things looked all right after awhile. I said how long awhile? He said let's say a few years. Three years or something. I said all right, I swear.

Thursday 19 of August.

Mother arrived yesterday with a suitcase. She says Aunt Susanne blew her lid over the adoption papers, but Mother told her she didn't want to hear it. "I told her you were *my* child and *I* was deciding," Mother said, and laughed like a child herself. "So now she's not talking to me. But that won't last a week.

"I've been thinking. Things are going to change at

home. I don't want that Pierre-Antoine anywhere near our house. Ever."

"Mother, don't be like that," I said. "Please, Mother. It's as much my fault as his."

"You seem to forget he's much older than you and has certain responsibilities."

I started to cry then, too. It just all seemed so cruel and pointless.

"All right," she said quickly. "All right. We'll talk about it. Don't cry."

It's incredible but she actually looked strong when she said this, and I believed her.

"We're going to do things together, just you and me. For example, I was thinking. The Pyramids. You've always wanted to go, haven't you? Well, at Christmas, we'll go. And schools. You hate that girls' lycée don't you? Well, there are so many lycées in Paris. Pick your school."

"A lycée that has boys," I said.

"Right. And I was thinking, maybe I'll get a job. You know that art gallery my friend owns? She's been asking me to work for her for years. How frightening!" She clapped her hands above her head. "It's like going to school for the first time!"

Then she got all serious. Her face turned pale and sad.

"Listen to me. This isn't going to be easy. It's going to hurt. Let me tell you about it . . ."

Mother has rented another room in Benoit's mother's house. So now she's here but she's not in my room all the time.

There are two things I can't stop thinking about. One, that soon it will be over and I can't wait to be free. Two, that I'm going to feel incredible pain. How am I supposed to act? What do they expect of me? Will I scream like women do in the movies? Will it scream for me, its mother, the way they do? What will I do then? I can't seem to find courage anywhere. It is like a black hole, a haunted house, a nightmare that is there all the time that I can't get away from. They say breathe deeply when you panic, breathe deeply and think with a clear head. I am trying to think with a clear head but I feel like peeing all the time from nerves.

Saturday 21 of August.

Benoit called the pastry shop and said he had a relapse of his flu. He told them he was pretty sure he'd be sick for a few days.

It's any time now, already a week late.

Benoit told me and Mother about when his mother had him. She was alone here in Trouville and walked to the hospital by herself. Her parents didn't talk to her for five years. Benoit remembers going when he was five to see his grandparents in Rouen for the first time. His mother just took him on the train and together they went and rang the doorbell of his grandparents' house. His grandmother lifted him up, held him pressed to her chest and cried.

This is supposed to be a wonderful moment in somebody's life. Everybody gathers around and gives you presents and tells you congratulations. It's not supposed to be like an operation where they're taking a huge cancer out of your stomach and everybody's whispering all the time. That's what I feel like. Like I'm dying of cancer and no one wants to admit it or talk about it with me.

Mother and Benoit have been trying so hard, though. They're so embarrassed, so touchy about it. They're my private family now. My public family is everyone else who is somehow connected to me.

Thursday 26 of August. Paris.

It happened on Sunday 22 of August. It started at dawn but didn't happen until about twelve hours later.

I feel like a glass bomb exploded inside of me. I am filled with pieces of glass. And my skin! Oh my God. The marks are like purple rivers and mountain chains on a map.

They kept me for three days. Everyone was really nice. Benoit came to visit every day and stayed for hours. We were laughing because at the hospital they think the baby is his. Benoit will be coming to Paris in a year and Mother has already found him a free room in an apartment building that her friend owns.

They gave me some kind of drug so it seems like a weird dream where I'm being interrogated and there are big lights everywhere. The doctor told me I'll be perfectly normal. All fixed up like it was before, he says. But what about my skin? I asked him. What about your skin? he says.

Aunt Susanne says Mother fainted when they took the little boy away. Aunt Susanne says he's blond and blue-eyed but that can change, she says, sometimes.

On the papers I put Benoit Antoine Phillippe for *First Names*. It says my name for *Mother* and then it says unemployed for *Profession*. Under *Father* I put unknown.

My God I'm so sorry. I pray someone will love him the way he deserves, the way I probably never could. I hope he'll want to find me some day. I hope to God I'm doing the right thing. I hope to God he grows up proud and strong.